OHIO READIN... BOOK

Grade 7

1980-81

Willow Whip

Willow Whip

by Irene Bennett Brown

Atheneum · New York
1979

LIBRARY OF CONGRESS CATALOGING IN PUBLICATION DATA

Brown, Irene Bennett.   Willow whip.

SUMMARY: In 1918 in Kansas a young girl is determined
to make it possible for her constantly moving,
tenant farmer family to buy a farm
that she has come to love
and wants to live on permanently.
[1. Family life—Fiction.   2. Farm life—Fiction]
I. Title.
PZ7.B81387Wi   [Fic]   79-11725
ISBN 0-689-30703-9

Published simultaneously in Canada by
McClelland & Stewart, Ltd.
Manufactured by
R. R. Donnelley & Sons, Crawfordsville, Indiana
Designed by Mary M. Ahern
First Edition

For

VESTA   HELBERG   BENNETT

My Mother

Willow Whip

one

THIRTEEN-year-old Willow Sabrina Faber stood in the doorway of the old stone barn where, last night, she had made a wish on a star. This morning, late May, 1918, she watched the warming sun flood gold onto the weathered farmhouse, cottonwood grove, and far-flung fields. The wish feeling came back, so strong she clamped her lips to keep from yelling what she longed for to the whole wide world.

Did they have to be movers all their lives? Finally, a husky whisper escaped her set mouth, "I want to stay here! I've got to find a way." She would be fourteen in July. Wasn't that long enough to be a nobody from nowhere?

Old Jingles, the family dog, crept from the crimson peonies that nodded in the wind alongside the gray frame house. Willow took her hands from the pockets of Papa's patched overalls and whistled the brown dog to her. She gave him his morning loving and remembered when they had come here in March—Papa driving one mule-drawn wagonload of belongings, Mama the other, with the youngest children sandwiched in here and there.

Willow, riding Eagle, and her younger brother, Walsh, on Papa's Dulcie, with Jingles' help, had driven their four milk cows and the calves. From the first moment of arriving Willow had had a feeling of belonging, a sense of coming home at last, about this farm they had rented. It was not just one more Kansas farm, to her it was *The Ranch*.

"You know, boy," she whispered now to the dog, "it would have been something to have lived on The Ranch when it was a stagecoach and pony express stop, a long, long time ago. The well, see, right there a few steps north of the house? That well gave up cold pure water to weary folk traveling through this Kansas country in the early days. Up there," Willow pointed above them to the wooden loft of the barn, "hewn timbers still got the mark of a real pioneer's broad axe!"

Stay, every stick, stone, and blade of grass seemed to say, although The Ranch had not looked like the end of the rainbow when they first came. Ancient, mountainous manure piles had had to be cleared from the barnyards. Uncaring earlier tenants had left the fields choked with quack grass and Canadian thistle, though now the fields were flourishing with young stands of corn and wheat. Willow's chin lifted. Sure, the house and privy and other outbuildings all leaked when it rained. "Papa'll get to them," she told the dog.

Willow's glance traveled to the pasture. Her blue eyes glowed, and she felt a warm rush of love, seeing her white pony Eagle grazing contentedly with the big mules, Jen and Ben. Eagle had been hers since she was very small, and riding the pony was her favorite pastime. Nearby was Dulcie, Papa's riding horse. Papa'd had the bay, Dulcie, for years, bought her when he came to America with his French bride. On the far side of the pasture Willow could make out Papa's stooped, barely moving form, so tiny from this distance. Papa'd been up for hours working on the fence that was lacy with gaping holes.

Willow gave Jingles a final hug. "Got to hurry," she said. The cows were milked but she must turn them out into the pasture and shovel out the barn—Walsh's chore, but he had made an excuse to go to the house early to be ready for school. Beyond the open barn door as Willow worked, a meadowlark trilled a clear, tuneful song. In the grove, where the fowl spent their nights bunched along tree limbs, a rooster crowed. These pleasant sounds were suddenly blotted out by a blood-curdling scream from the direction of the house. Willow froze; her heart beat faster. What—?

The screaming continued, growing, multiplying. Willow yanked the back barn door shut and threw the shovel toward a corner. Someone needed help for some reason. She stumbled in her oversized work shoes as she ran through the barn.

Outside, she saw her nine-year-old brother, Adan, hopping and jumping about the yard with the vicious bill of Chandler, Mama's young gray goose, clamped to the seat of his overalls; the goose's orange splayed feet seldom touched ground. Cowering behind the well wall, emitting ear-splitting yells but doing little else to help their younger brother, squatted ten-year-old Walsh, and Jessamyn, eleven. School books and papers flapped in the yard. Old Jingles, tail tucked under, raced across the field toward infinity. Dumb scared dog is as bad as Walsh and Jessy, Willow thought fleetingly.

She snatched up a rake that leaned against the barn and rushed at the goose still nipping at Adan's backside. "Shoo!" she yelled, "scat, you ornery goose!" For a second, Willow believed that Chandler was going to turn on her. Instead, he took off in a fluttering run for the cottonwood grove, hoarse *ga ga ga*'s tearing from his throat. The rest of the barnyard geese and chickens fluttered noisily after him.

Trembling and sweaty, Willow put the rake away. She hurried to Adan, and after a slight hesitation, drew the boy's skinny shoulders into the circle of her arm. As he looked up at her, his blue eyes filled with fresh tears. His light brown hair was wild, and his normally ruddy face was pale and wet. "It's all right, Chandler is gone," Willow soothed.

Adan nodded. His chin started to quiver and he clamped his lips tight.

Walsh joined them, his chubby face about to break into a grin. Willow glared. "You were sure brave!" Walsh's glance dropped, but his husky shoulders twitched with held-in laughter. "You, too." Willow turned angrily on Jessamyn who was gathering books and papers from the ground.

"What could I do?" Jessamyn protested. "That looney goose might have torn my good dress." She tossed her head prettily; her sandy hair rippled in neat waves to her shoulders. After a moment, Jessamyn said, "I'm sorry, Adan. Walsh is—you're sorry, too, aren't you! Oh, this is wasting time. Willow, it's time for us to leave for school and you smell like the barn."

Barn smell was natural to Willow's way of thinking, and not so bad. To tell the truth, she seldom noticed it. She grinned at Jessy, who was crinkling her thin little nose, and shrugged. "I'll be ready, don't worry, and I'll smell sweet enough to suit even you, Queen Of Sheba. Laurel isn't here"— Willow looked around for their seven-year-old sister—"and the rest of you don't have your dinner pails that I can see." Grumbling to each other, Walsh, Jessamyn, and Adan trailed Willow across the rickety porch, back into the house.

At the red-checked oilcloth-covered table in the kitchen, Mama spooned oatmeal into baby Mitty in her highchair. A cute mite, Willow thought, even with dabs of mush in her tangle of blonde curls. On Mama's other side four-year-old Clay, another curlyhead, appeared to be drowning himself in a glass of milk. Distracted by Willow and the others' entrance, Mama held the full spoon in midair, while Mitty leaned farther and farther forward, her rosebud mouth opening wider and wider.

"You were fighting again, eh?" Mama asked tiredly, her hand going up to smooth the silvery tendrils that had escaped from the dark bun at the back of her head. "What make the fuss this time?"

"Chandler!" the older ones answered in unified disgust.

Adan, his fright on the wane, was furious. "I get me a Daisy Air Rifle, that Chandler's gonna get it." He sniffed.

Willow nodded. "Chandler's a no-good goose. If we had golden geese that would lay golden eggs, that'd be different. Then we could own this place."

"*Pardon!*" Mama mocked Willow, her eyebrows shooting up, a touch of fire in her eyes. "You think big, *chérie*. Own, eh? Buy Ranch, *oui*. So easy, you think? My geese, you forget maybe, and pay from goose eggs, plain goose eggs, do most care for family!" Mama was spooning now a bit too fast, but like a little snapping turtle, Mitty was keeping up.

Willow sighed. What was wrong with wanting The Ranch for themselves? Couldn't the others see how good it would be for them all, to stay here, right here, always? Of course finding golden goose eggs wasn't the way, but there must be something they could do. She couldn't, wouldn't, give up. The hand pump at the sink clanked and gasped as Willow pumped water into a speckled basin. She washed hastily and dried her face and hands on a flour-sack towel. "Do I have a clean dress?"

Mama answered, a studying look still in her eyes as she faced Willow, "The blue flour sack print, she is clean."

Wonderful, wonderful flour sacks. Willow didn't say it out loud, knowing better than to rile her mother further. Plain flour sacks became dish towels, towels, and diapers. Six of them sewed together made a sheet, or tablecloth, take your pick. Printed ones, of course, were made into clothes. Make do. Their entire lives were *make do*.

But . . . this dress is kind of nice, Willow decided, buttoning the bodice as she came from the back bedroom. Bright, tiny blue flowers bloomed on white, and Mama had cleverly added a big white collar and wide, snug belt. Willow peeked into the blotchy mirror by the back door and felt even better. The dress looked good with her dark brown hair and it made her light blue eyes seem violet. "Where's Laurel?" Willow asked, gathering up her books and lard-bucket dinner pail from the table.

"Eh?" Mama looked puzzled. "She went out . . ." Mama nodded. "In privy," she said with a shake of her head. "You look."

Willow laughed. "Laurel's afraid to come out. That fuss with Chandler. We'll stop for her on our way. Jessamyn, grab Laurel's dinner pail."

Jessy gave Willow a look that warned not to get too bossy, but did as she was told.

Hurrying along the worn path to the small building, Willow could hear the little first-grader inside singing to herself, or maybe to her ever-present doll, Amanda. "Willow will come and get me, yes she will, yes she will," the faint voice singsonged. "Willow will come and save us, and the bad old goose will run, run away. Away, awaaay—"

So as to not hurt the little girl's feelings, Willow kept laughter from her voice, "Come out, Laurel, we're going to be late for school."

The small girl's eyes were adoring as she came out and put her hand in Willow's. "I thought Indians were scap-ting Adan, but it was just Chandler, huh?" She hugged her doll closer under her arm, but then the dark-haired, china-faced doll's sawdust heart was never far from Laurel's own human heart.

"Just Chandler. I thought it was Indians, too." Willow quickly smoothed Laurel's short, wispy hair, and wondered if Mama had noticed this morning how Laurel's eyes were so dark underneath. "Feel like running?" Willow asked.

"Sure."

Neither Willow nor the others suggested Laurel leave Amanda home. It wouldn't have done any good.

Old Jingles came loping up to see them off, his tail wagging, his head ducked in shame at being afraid of Chandler. They ordered him to stay and set out on the usual back route to Johncreek School, Walsh and Adan leading the way along the blind lane, or wagon ruts, that followed the fence line.

Looking back, Willow saw that Clay had come out of the house and looked as if he, too, might try to follow. She called to him to stay home and for answer, the tot solemnly stooped, picked up a handful of dirt, and threw it after them.

As she hurried along, Willow snugged her belt tighter, and sniffed the back of her hand to be sure she smelled like soap and not the barn. She checked the skirt of her dress for wrinkles. *Hope Reid Evans likes blue.* Willow stumbled in the dusty path. Where on earth did that idea come from? she wondered. It had slipped into her mind like a silly lost butterfly. It had landed in the wrong head! If she wasn't careful, she'd be as fussy about the way she looked as her sister Jessy!

Oh, fiddle, Willow gave in, it'd take a woodenhead dumbbell not to notice Reid, the best-looking boy in her class. "Jessy," Willow spoke aloud, "wouldn't you like to live here on The Ranch from now on, go to this school long enough to make good friends, true-lasting friends?" She didn't say *and have a beau, maybe, too,* but she was thinking it.

Walking slightly ahead, Jessy turned and looked at Willow. "Ain't no use to get your hopes up," Jessamyn said with a shake of her head. Her lips parted and her almost perfect teeth caught her bottom lip; she shook her head again. "No use to want what we can't have. Something'll come up, like it always does, and we'll be moving on next year."

Willow felt like arguing, but held her tongue. Jessy gave in too easy. The trouble was, Jessy and the younger ones didn't remember what it was like to be stayers. She did. For six happy years they had lived on the same farm in Ellsworth County where she was born. When Papa got the farm built up real good, the owner took it back, wanting to run it then, himself.

They'd moved every year since. Mostly, she guessed, because the best farms around had permanent, live-on owners, but there might be other reasons. In his talk, it seemed Papa always moved them with the hope of finding better than they had. Papa'd never find better than The Ranch, to her way of thinking. If they could stay on The Ranch, again have a piece of earth they could truly feel was *home*, like the Ellsworth County place—how wonderful that would be!

Willow sighed, feeling forlorn, but not beaten, yet.

To their right, a short while later, lay the town of Seena—a honeycomb cluster of buildings hugging the flat, sunny plain. As they neared the town, the Fabers could see a woman battling the hot morning wind to hang a sheet on her clothesline; in another backyard a small child staggered sleepily toward the outhouse. From the center of town came the bustling rattle of wagon wheels, and a lone *"oogah"* of an auto horn. The garbled voices of businessmen, calling to one another as they unlocked their doors, carried on the wind.

Laurel was having a hard time keeping up. Willow wordlessly handed her things to Jessamyn, hoisted the small girl and her doll onto her back, and hurried on.

The schoolbell clanged just as Willow and Laurel followed the others in a last breathless spurt across the schoolyard. They separated quickly, inside. Panting, Willow dashed to her own room and dropped into her backrow seat. It was some seconds before she caught on that Miss Barnes had departed from her usual strict schedule of flag salute, prayer, singing, then arithmetic, and instead was leading a discussion about next week's last day of school picnic.

"My father," Farley Baxter was saying with a wave of his plump hand, "will donate cakes—coconut layer cake, chocolate fudge, a Lady Baltimore cake, too." The glance of his keen blue eyes swept the room as though to learn if he had set mouths watering. The baker's son plopped back into his seat looking pleased.

At a nod from Miss Barnes, Jarma Walbridge stood up and adjusted the wire-rimmed spectacles that clung precariously to her wide, flat face. "I'll see that a notice about the picnic is written up in the *Seena Bugle*." Only recently had Willow learned that Jarma's father was editor of the *Bugle*.

Willow experienced a hollow feeling inside that was like pain as she listened to the others. What was it like to be one of the lucky few with front row desks, making plans for everyone? In the no-end of schools she'd gone to, it was always the same—the Fabers, and other children of tenant farmers who moved each year, were back-of-the-room students. As though by some rule nobody ever spoke aloud, they were never truly a part. It was something she did not like and vowed time and again to change.

"We will need a donation of a small farm animal to be auctioned off to raise money for the Red Cross war effort, as other schools are doing," Willow heard Miss Barnes saying.

Startled, Willow realized that her hand was raised.

"Willow Faber?" Miss Barnes looked a bit vexed at the interruption. "Do you need to leave the room?"

"No. No, I don't. I want to volunteer—I want to give—a prime young gander—goose—to be auctioned for—for the war ef-effort." When it was all said, Willow felt faint. Poor Chandler. And Mama and Papa would—!

"Ohhh?" Miss Barnes drew out. "All right. Yes. Willow Faber has promised a goose for our auction."

Willow could feel every eye on her. A buzzing rose in the room. Miss Barnes cleared her throat. "Ahhh. We must hurry on. Melinda Lewis?"

Melinda Kay Lewis, a fluffy-haired blonde in a pretty, store-bought dress, stood and faced the class. "My mama and her friends will bring their special dishes, and they will serve, of course," she said primly. "Papa expected to buy a little pig to give for the lottery, to help Mama, since she is president of the Seena Red Cross Chapter. But, since she"—Melinda nodded at Willow—"promised a—a goose, well . . . ."

The snickering that followed was directed at her, Willow knew. She carefully studied the inkwell on her desk while an unwelcome warmth crawled up her throat. Melinda's father was Seena's only banker and sure could have afforded to buy the pig. Was *that* the difference, did your Pa have to be an important businessman for a person to count? Conroy Gill's papa owned the livery and wagon works. Reid Evans's mother ran the boarding house. Anger stirred in Willow. Papa, if they only knew him, Papa was the kindest—and a good farmer, too, and . . . Willow's thoughts were ended abruptly when Reid Evans leaped to his feet.

The tall, straw-haired boy's hazel eyes twinkled with good humor.

"Reid? You have something to offer?" From the look on Miss Barnes's face, Reid had her charmed like everyone else, Willow thought, her own anger mellowing.

"Yes'm." Reid laughed. "I want the girls to

know," he opened his arms wide, "that I'll be at the picnic to show 'em a good time." His chuckle was deep as he danced a shuffling jig around his desk.

Willow laughed with the others.

"Hey, a fly!" Conroy Gill, showing off, pointed to a speck of black on his desk. He reached with care for a dictionary that lay by his other hand, then let the three-pound book drop with a thunderous boom.

"Enough. Enough," Miss Barnes scolded. "That will do, meeting adjourned."

In midafternoon, Willow's book lay open on her desk, the words danced meaninglessly before her eyes. Her stomach felt queasy. What would Mama and Papa do tonight, when she told them she had promised to give away their valuable goose? If you had plenty, like the Lewises, Baxters, and Reids— that was different. What had gotten into her?

two

WITH her elbows propped on either side of her book, Willow stared unseeing at the page, then her worried frown eased into a smile. The others in class had noticed her today. If the Fabers kept The Ranch, stayed on the way she hoped, next fall she might be able to go to high school, to the new academy on the northwest edge of town. A happy shiver raced along her spine. Being a two-year person here, she might get a front row seat!

"Willow Faber, you may close your geography." Miss Barnes's voice cut sharply into Willow's reverie. "This is health period and we are discussing typhoid fever. Did you read your assignment?"

Willow's face burned. "Y-yes, Miss Barnes," she mumbled, "I read it." She closed the geography and took out her health book, flipping the pages with nervous fingers.

"What did you learn from the chapter on typhoid fever? Can you tell us the symptoms, Willow? The diagnosis, what causes typhoid fever?" Miss Barnes pressed.

Willow nodded thoughtfully. "I can tell what

the book said, and I can tell what it is really like. My little sister Laurel had typhoid fever last spring." The room noise faded into quiet.

"That is unfortunate, but I am glad you can tell us firsthand about typhoid. What did your parents notice first, when Laurel became ill?"

"*I* knew it first, that she was sick, Laurel was with me," Willow answered. Encouraged by a nod from Miss Barnes, she continued, "We lived on a farm near Wistalia last year, a terrible, dirty, run-down place. I had taken the team and wagon, and my sisters and brothers, to a wild plum thicket to pick fruit for Mama to make jam. Laurel was starting fights and crying, all day. Most times she is the best-natured little kid in the world. When it came time to go home she was . . . she was too weak to climb into the wagon. I lifted her up—she was hot as a furnace."

"Go on," Miss Barnes said softly. She brought her chair from in back of her desk and sat down with her hands in her lap.

"When I got Laurel home, Mama noticed right off that Laurel's stomach was all puffed up. Laurel hurt all over. Mama said, 'It's typhoid.' She sent me to Wistalia on my pony Eagle to get Leafy." Willow explained, "Leafy Jennings is a young black lady who knows how to do for people bad sick. There weren't any real doctors around. Like now, most of them were gone to the war to take care of soldiers." Willow drew a deep breath. "It was a hot day, hard to breathe, even. I—I almost killed my pony Eagle riding so hard for Leafy."

"What did Leafy Jennings do for your sister?" Melinda Kay asked with interest.

Surprised, Willow hesitated, then told her, "She gave Laurel cool baths, one right after another, to get her fever down. Medicine didn't help, but good clear soup helped her feel better. Leafy put her in a room alone—we couldn't go in, and Mama worked night and day to disinfect bedding, and clothes, and dishes. Everything was boiled in carbolic acid. They couldn't do anything to sterilize her dolly; Papa had to burn it." Willow sighed, remembering, then went on, "It was our job, my brothers' and sister's and mine, to kill flies, and it was a bad year for them—they were thick, black, everywhere." Willow shuddered, remembering.

"Did you get to see Laurel at all? What did she look like, sick?" Farley Baxter was curious.

"At first I saw her. She got weaker and weaker. It—it was so ugly. Laurel had nosebleeds, a rash, she couldn't talk or move, hardly. Everybody thought she would—would die." Willow swallowed. "Laurel got to be skin and bones, she lost her hair. After a long time, months, she started getting better, although she isn't all the way over what typhoid did to her, yet. We got her a new doll that she won't hardly never put down, for anything." Willow added, "They say I—I saved my little sister's life, going so fast for Leafy, on Eagle. But it was Leafy, and Mama; they just wouldn't give up."

Miss Barnes spoke after a long silence, "We know from our book that typhoid fever is a disease of the intestines. It is caused by drinking polluted water or milk, or by eating spoiled food. The great typhoid epidemics in history have been traced to sewage-polluted water. As you know from Willow's story, these outbreaks don't always take place in large cities. Willow, did your family learn how Laurel got typhoid?"

Willow shrank in her seat, her throat constricted. How could she answer this hated question? Blood climbed to her face and her eyes flashed. "I'll tell you! In the country it is *filth*. It is flies. It is privies built practically on top of the wells we drink from. That's what causes typhoid."

It was a struggle to slow her anger, her humiliation. She wanted to tell them that what she had just said fit almost every tenant farm in the land. Except The Ranch with its beautiful deep well many yards from the privy. Her voice lowered as she finished, "Laurel had some water in a jar in her little playhouse; the playhouse was some boards leaned against a tree. She drank from that jar. We don't know. But maybe that gave her typhoid fever."

There was a kindly glow in Miss Barnes's eyes. "Thank you, Willow. None of us are safe from typhoid in these times. Because of what you shared with the people in this room, they, at least, will be more conscious of good hygiene habits. We can all work toward putting an end to this dreadful disease."

Willow made an effort to smile, appreciating Miss Barnes's praise, but her thoughts had skipped from the schoolroom and were on Papa. If she could get Papa to listen to her as this class had today, she might be able to make him see that they had to stop moving around from one ramshackle tenant farm to the next. What happened to Laurel wasn't the only good reason. For her, and the others must have felt it too, everywhere they'd been the past few years, she'd had this awful feeling of having no home, of being *nobody.*

Could she explain that to Papa? Would he pay her any heed, see how important it was?

After school, Willow trailed the younger ones home, deep in thought. She didn't know why Papa'd never struck out on his own; she only knew that since his arrival from Sweden years before she was born, he had always worked for others. First as a farmhand, then a farmer on rented land—sometimes sharing crops to pay the rent, though he'd rather pay cash rent after selling what he raised. She shook her head, clasping tighter to her chest the tattered farm magazine.

The magazine was several months old, donated to Johncreek School by Melinda Kay's family. Willow asked if she could have it, feeling a reverence she might have felt for an original copy of the

Declaration of Independence because there was an account in the magazine that would convince Papa it was possible to buy The Ranch. She just knew it!

First, she had to tell what she had done about Chandler, she decided, feeling uneasy.

"You what!" Papa cried at supper, lowering his chunk of cornbread back to his plate. "Julie!" His slight wiry figure turned in the chair toward Willow's mother. "You hear what our girl tell us? She gave away for nothing a goose worth two or three dollars!" Papa raked his hand back through his graying yellow hair and yanked his drooping moustache.

Willow needed no clearer sign to tell her that Papa, a kind, mild-eyed man usually, was angry. Willow gnawed her lip, unable to look Papa in the face any longer. She saw Mama nod "yes," then shake her head "no" repeatedly. Then Mama took a deep breath, and plunged, "Y-you right, Karl, but— is Willow not right, too? Money from Chandler will buy bandages and medicine for poor young men who risk the lives in my homeland, France. For us, too, they are fight. Willow want us to be part of neighborhood, help USA, too. Is that not good, eh? *Bien, bien,* is right." Mama looked imploringly at Papa, her long-fingered hands clasped tight before her on the table.

Mama's speech surprised Willow. "Thanks, Mama," Willow said after a second, a relieved grin spreading across her face. She had had no idea Mama would feel this way. She hoped Mama could see just how much she thanked her. From the corner of her eye, Willow saw that Papa's anger was fading, but being Papa, he had to pretend otherwise awhile longer.

"All right," he said, "all right about the goose. Just remember who is head of this house. What is two, three dollars, anyway? Give it away, *yah*," he grumbled. Around the table the members of his family tried to look solemn while their eyes danced with glee.

This is a good time—now or never, Willow decided. "Papa," she began slowly, "you're a top-notch farmer." It wouldn't hurt to make Papa feel good, and anyway, it was true. "Mama says even in Sweden when you farmed ten rocky acres, you were the best. You—you ought to have your own place, Papa. Please"—she took a deep breath—"please —let's buy this ranch!"

Papa's jaw sagged. "Buy?" he asked after a moment, "Buy again is it!" His fork fell with a clatter by his plate. He looked at Willow as though he could not believe she would suggest such an insane thing.

"Yes, Papa, buy," Willow plunged on recklessly. "Every February you go away on Dulcie looking for a different farm to rent on shares. Every March we all have to throw out, pick up, bid good-bye to people we never hardly got to know, anyway, and move on to another rented farm that isn't any better than the one before. Some of them have been plain awful, like where we lived when Laurel got sick, till we fixed them up, Papa. The Ranch is the best we've seen in a long time. Let's stay here, turn this place into the best farm in Kansas. It could be like the one in Ellsworth County where we lived a long time when I was little. I know we could, Papa—"

"Listen to this!" Papa interrupted, "a little girl talking about owning land." Papa's moustache twitched like golden butterflies in a wind. "I just never heard the like. Listen, young smart mouth, I tell you. If we don't own the farm, in a bad year we don't lose it from foreclosure. Farming on shares is good. I pay rent to owners from money we get from crops we raise. Rest of cash pays grocery man for what we got to have but can't grow, and for clothes. Sometimes we get a little profit, too, sometimes. *Yah*, I would like to own farm. But I say let the landlords, them Abraham brothers, worry. Let them have the headache of taxes and all that."

"Awww, Papa! You'll work yourself near to death on this place," Willow wailed, "work me, too. For what? For somebody else like always." She slid down in her chair, then came up fast, alarmed, when she saw Papa's face. A crimson thundercloud seemed to be breaking there. He reached across the table and wagged a finger under her nose. "Papa, Papa, I'm sorry, but—please—we could—"

"Go to bed," he ordered. "To bed. You don't talk back like this to your Papa." He waved a hand toward the bedroom Willow shared with Jessamyn and Laurel. For a long, awful moment, there wasn't a sound from the others at the table; then baby Mitty began to cry, mopping her blue eyes with wet chubby fists, looking around her with worry.

"I—I'm sorry, Papa." Willow pushed back from the table, feeling washed out, angry at herself. She should have talked to Papa more carefully. She had ruined it all with her own big mouth. "Good night," she said huskily. At the door to her room, Willow threw Papa a half-hopeful look. Maybe, if she talked more—man to man? His stony countenance stopped her. And Mama looked too upset. Better keep your mouth still, for now, Willow decided with regret.

Willow undressed in the dark, got into her nightgown, and crawled into her blankets, her eyes growing bleary with tears. "Oh, Papa," she whispered after a long time, "if only I could make you know how I feel. I'm scared inside, of being rootless, Papa. I don't feel we were intended to live no-account like tumbling tumbleweeds or something. But I feel no-account, and I don't like it at all. It's not me. Here and now, please God, I want to get to be somebody. And I'm not afraid to work for it." Weren't folks supposed to *become* not just *be?*"

At last Willow fell into a light, uneasy sleep. She stirred and was vaguely aware that Jessamyn and Laurel were getting into the other bed, sometime later.

SUDDENLY, someone was shaking her shoulder hard. "Willow! Wake up, wake up!" came Mama's soft cry. "What is matter with you?"

Willow struggled to come to a sitting position and couldn't. Her eyelids felt welded shut, her lips would not form the words she was trying to say. A heavy feeling of dread and sadness seemed to hold her down. She wet her lips and tried to remember, then fought the whimper that rose swiftly in her throat. "M-Mama?" Willow managed to say, thickly, "I—I had a d-dream, a nightmare." She wiped at the moisture beaded on her forehead. "I—I keep having it."

"You make terrible noise," Mama scolded lightly. "But you don't wake other chil'ren, yet. Go back to sleep, *chérie*."

"Wait!" Willow grabbed Mama's arm. "Please," she whispered. "I've had this dream before, off and on since I was six or seven. I—I have to tell you." She pulled herself up as Mama hesitated. With both hands on Mama's arm, Willow brought her mother down to sit on the bed beside her.

"The n-nightmare is so—awful." Willow's voice caught. "We're in it, all us Fabers. Only—only in the nightmare we are—are yellow rosebushes. I know that sounds silly, but that's what we are, beautiful rosebushes. At—at first we're beautiful. Then—then each year we get yanked up, our feet, our roots, out of the ground, and moved. Until f-finally"—a shiver raced through Willow—"we wither and d-die. We're blown away in the dust, never heard of again. Or, ever remembered by—by anyone."

The room seemed to have gone cold. Mama stroked Willow's bare arm, smoothing away the chill bumps there. "I know, daughter," Mama whispered. "I worry, too. No roots, is not good for my chil'ren. I—I wan' to stay put, too, ver' much, but—"

"Then help me, Mama, help me make Papa see that we got to stay where we are," Willow begged. "Papa must care. But why does he keep moving us? Is—is he restless, the times we could stay, doesn't he want to settle down?"

"*Non*, not that," Mama was quick to say. "Is many reasons, but Papa care. Except for time or two, like on farm where you were born, Papa never find place he think good enough for his family. Always, he look for better."

Willow nodded slowly, understanding.

After a silence, Mama continued, and her voice was warm with the love and respect she felt for Papa. "Karl, he decide what best for family. You want me to tell your Papa what to do, eh?" Mama said. "Wear his trousers, too, eh? No, my *chérie*, Papa is head of house. Crowing from fencepost isn't work for hen, it is rooster's work, remember that."

Mama gave Willow's arm a last pat. "*C'est la vie—* that is life. Go to sleep."

Mama wasn't going to be any help persuading Papa, Willow realized with a sinking heart. She rested on her elbow and listened to Mama's fading footfalls. Go back to sleep? She trembled. If she went to sleep, the nightmare might come back. Willow lay and stared wide-eyed into the thick, soft dark, thinking. Even if Mama wanted to go against Papa, she wouldn't. In every other thing she would want it that way, Willow thought, Mama and Papa like one in their doing. But this time. . . .

If only she hadn't riled Papa right off in their talk, she could have shown him the piece in the farm magazine. She was sure Papa would have at least given it careful thought. She had to try again in the morning, Willow decided. In spite of Mama's warning about roosters and hens and their places in life, she had to take a chance.

With that thought, Willow's muscles gradually relaxed and after a while she was again asleep.

A gray light filtered through the window when Willow next opened her eyes, blinking. Won't be long until the sun is up, she realized, snuggling deeper into her blankets. Remembering, now, she was glad she hadn't suffered the awful nightmare a second time in the night. Only thinking of it brought a sick feeling to her stomach. Blessed nightmare, anyway! How she hated it! Willow threw back her blanket and, shaking, got into her barn clothes—

green plaid shirt, faded, raggedy overalls, and heavy high-top shoes.

She had nearly finished milking Annie, her second cow of the morning, when she felt Papa's hand light gently on her shoulder. "Daughter." Papa cleared his throat. "I'm sorry I yell at you last night. You been a good help to your Papa, *yah*, sure, almost from the time you step out of your cradle. Riding the plow horse to guide it, milking cows when you was just a little girl, and sowing seed as good as a man, *yah*. I see it is no wonder you get notion to own a place, ourselves. But we can't, daughter, we just can't."

Papa was seeing her side, dogged if he wasn't! Was he weakening too, maybe willing to hear more? "Papa," Willow said, her heart beating fast as she looked up to give him a thankful smile, "I've been finding out some things, things you ought to know. Let me tell you, please?" She ignored the sudden squint of Papa's left eye that meant he did not want to hear.

"Because of the war," Willow plunged on, "because of the enormous need for food in Europe, prices for crops are the best they have ever been, Papa. It can't last—twenty dollars for a hog, two and a quarter dollars for a bushel of wheat, a dollar seventy-five a bushel of corn." She took a deep breath and continued. "They say prices will go back down after the war is over. I read something, Papa: *Out in Kansas or Oklahoma a man who gets two good crops*

of wheat at this year's prices can buy a farm. The
time to buy a farm is right now, Papa, and the farm
we ought to get is right here, The Ranch."

Willow didn't know that her tan strong fingers
worked in vigorous accompaniment to her words
until Annie tossed her head and gave a throaty *moo*
of protest. Willow let up. She could feel the blood
pounding in her ears as she waited for Papa's answer.
He must understand, he just had to want this too.
She looked up at him, scarcely breathing.

Papa's small, craggy face was serious, unsmiling
behind his moustache, doubt plain in his pale blue
eyes. After what seemed forever Papa voiced his
thoughts out loud. "Such hard work it would take.
But you make me think, since last night. Your Mama
tell me about bad dream." Papa stroked his moustache and shook his head. "Just you and me to do
the work, Walsh helping us. *Nay,* I don't think we
could do it."

He was giving in, he was! "We could, Papa.
Oh, yes, we could." Willow leaped to her feet, the
three-legged milking stool went tumbling. She stead-
ied the pail of ivory-colored milk, then hugged
Papa's wiry frame. "Papa, we can try, can't we? I
know we can do it. I'll work harder. I'll make the
other kids work harder. We will earn money every
which way under the sun until we have a down payment to put on The Ranch. It'll be ours, Papa, just
think of it—ours."

The soft light that settled in Papa's eyes, then,

was new to Willow, a reflection it seemed, of some long-buried dreams of Papa's own. After what seemed forever, he nodded. "We try. *Yah*, sure, we probably fail, but we try." He took Willow's arms down. "The milk sour, you stand here hugging your Papa so long."

Willow grinned, grabbed the milking stool, and sat down to strip the last drops of Annie's warm milk into the pail. "Mama's going to like this, Papa, hearing you say that you've decided to stay here." Looking ahead in her mind, Willow could hardly wait to see Mama's reaction to Papa's announcement of this near-miracle.

three

SHE wanted never to forget this, not ever, Willow thought, watching in the kitchen when Papa broke the news, after chores. Mama threw back her head and laughed joyously, "We stay? We going to try to buy—how Willow say, so big, *The Ranch*?" Then Mama began to cry, her laughter all mixed in with tears while Papa held her and patted her shoulder.

Jessamyn clutched Laurel and her doll and they twirled about the crowded kitchen in a reckless waltz. Walsh, Adan, and four-year-old Clay buffeted one another in a noisy, three-way sparring match. Baby Mitty, in her high chair, burst into tears, wide-eyed at the others' odd behavior.

Willow, whose insides felt funny-soft as milkweed down, went to the baby, knelt, and untied her. Willow took Mitty up into her arms and buried her face in the sobbing baby's silken curls. Whispering into her ear, she said, "Know what I think? I think Mama and Papa have maybe always wanted to stay put. Maybe, honey, they needed us to come along and coax them into taking a chance."

* * *

FOLKS would think well of her from now on or she'd know the reason why, Willow decided, on the morning of the school picnic. She raced through chores, gobbled her buckwheat pancakes, then sneaked Jessamyn's special rose soap for a sponge bath in the bedroom. Humming to herself, she put on her too small but best dress, the yellow one with black polka dots, then slipped her stockinged feet into black patent shoes with worn, open cracks across the tops. She brushed her hair into shining brown waves. The Ranch, Seena, the schools, the land all around here would be her home forever more. She'd earn it; she'd belong, yes she would!

Mama's voice came through the closed door, interrupting Willow's thoughts, "What you do in there? Other chil'ren all go to school half hour ago."

"Drat. They did?" She'd meant for Walsh to carry Chandler to school for her; now she would have to do it, herself. Anyway, the goose was ready to go. He had given more trouble than she needed, after chores, before she finally got him into a burlap sack, which she tied shut with strong twine.

A short while later, alone, Willow followed the blind lane toward school, holding the heavy bundle that was Chandler out away from her dress. The goose was heavier than she thought he'd be. In no time, a fierce ache settled in her arms. Forced to give up trying to save her dress, Willow finally rested the squirming bundle on her hip. She cried out as Chandler jabbed his beak into her side. "Ouch!

Stop it." Willow slapped where she thought his head would be. Chandler, in the bag, struggled and set up a fierce honking.

As they came into distant view of Seena's back-yards, Willow tried to quiet the noisy goose. "Shhh," she begged in a whisper, "you'll have the whole town looking at us."

A pair of scraggly dogs nosed through some weeds about a junk pile in back of a shed some yards away. Willow eyed them warily and swal-lowed. "Please," she begged Chandler, "you got to quiet down. Please."

Chandler might have been trying to get even with her as he gabbled angrily and honked even louder. Willow's heart beat faster as the dogs, one black, the other dirty white, stopped suddenly, lifted their heads, and looked in her direction. Both animals were slat-thin, Willow saw. Hungry dogs.

The ugly creatures loped toward her, stopped, came on. Willow's steps quickened. "Don't," she begged under her breath, "don't bother us, please." The black dog trotted up to her side, sniffed at the burlap bag, then dodged out of range when Willow kicked. "Go away!" she ordered, "get!" The dogs began to circle her, yelping in wet-mouthed antici-pation. Chandler, quiet for a change, struggled so hard inside the bag it was all Willow could do to hang on to him.

The dirty white dog rushed in and nipped at the sack. Willow pulled her burden away and tried to run. "No," she cried, "you can't have him, go away." She swung the heavy bundle around in front of her and ran hard. The black dog, teeth bared, came after her, so close that Willow's nose was filled with strong dog smell and her skin crawled. Too late, she saw yellowed fangs catch at the old burlap, and heard the sack rip.

Sick now with fear, Willow found the tear and clutched the gap together with her fist. She yelled at the dog, kicked, stumbled, then regained her balance and ran on.

Looking, she saw Johncreek School ahead. Finally! She had to make it. If the dogs got Chandler they'd eat him in a flash. The dumb goose would be nothing but feathers after that, and the high-toned school bunch would really laugh at her.

As she ran, Willow felt a dog's frothing mouth on her thigh, through her dress, felt it nip her leg. "Oh, stop," she pleaded, "leave me alone." She looked hopefully toward the school but saw that the schoolyard was quiet, empty. She was late. Worse, there was nobody outside to see, to help her.

Both animals rushed in, Willow's feet tangled, she stumbled then caught herself in time. In that instant a tall figure stepped out of the building into the schoolyard. "Help," Willow croaked, "Miss Barnes, help me!" Willow saw the teacher turn, stiffen, then swing the bell in her hand, high.

Losing the battle to stay on her feet—against the leaping, lunging dogs, Willow went down with an agonized groan, holding her bundle as protectively as she could. She landed on her right shoulder with a thud. All around her the air was filled with horrid noise—angry gabbling and honking from Chandler, sharp yelps from the dogs, the *clang, clang* of Miss Barnes's bell. It was enough to bring the dead from their graves over to the Seena cemetery, Willow thought, hoping no one looked out the school window. She struggled to her knees and looked for the dogs, ready to dodge them if need be. She saw a black streak followed by a white streak flying back toward town. Willow sighed thankfully.

"Heavens to Betsy! Are you all right?" Miss Barnes asked, helping Willow to her feet.

"It doesn't matter a-about me," Willow panted, "but I guess I am. I reckon Chandler knows his goose is about cooked," she managed to joke. As she handed over the sack to Miss Barnes, Chandler poked his head through the hole and complained at the top of his goose lungs, until the teacher grabbed his head and beak to quiet him.

Willow brushed at the dust powdered into the fabric of her yellow polka-dot dress. The teacher's expression was mirror enough to tell her she looked a sight. Shaking her head, Willow breathed deep for courage and followed Miss Barnes into the schoolhouse. If this morning was a sign, this whole blessed day was going to be plain awful!

In spite of the squiggles of nervousness in her

stomach, Willow paid small heed to the giggles and pointing fingers of her classmates as she passed them. In the cloakroom she made an attempt to put herself to rights. On a bench just inside the door there was always a tall cream can filled with water. She took the dipper and ladled a splash of water into the tin basin placed by the can. She washed in a rush and with damp fingers fixed her hair. It would have to do. She went to her seat and pretended to be tidying up her desk, so she wouldn't have to see the others looking at her.

The sound of creaking wheels, muffled voices, and stamping hooves soon told that parents were arriving outside. Willow felt a pang of regret that Mama and Papa would not be among the parents. They had needed to stay home to work, but had urged Willow and the younger ones not to miss the picnic.

A short while later, a file of horse-drawn wagons filled with chattering school children rolled along West Main street, took a left turn at the tracks, then continued north another two miles to the picnic grove and pond.

Although she was weary from her tussle with the dogs, Willow soon caught the others' excitement, and her spirits rose. She stood up in the jolting wagon for a better look as they turned into the shady cluster of cottonwood and elm trees at the grounds. Boys and girls, her brothers and sisters among them, spilled from the halted wagons. Whooping and shouting, they spread colorfully every which way in the grove.

Some of the fathers were already there, putting planks on sawhorses for tables; others were pounding stakes into the ground for horseshoe pitching, while still others cleared debris from the well-worn baseball diamond. Willow again felt sorry that Mama and Papa stayed home.

Willow started and stepped out of the way as Reid, Melinda Kay, and Farley Baxter and Jarma raced past her to the yellow canoes beached at the pond's edge. Watching the two couples guide the canoes across the surface of the cool-looking green-brown water, Willow felt a tug of longing to be with them. But they hadn't asked her. She walked on.

Willow found Laurel looking on as a circle of first-graders played drop the handkerchief. Willow bent down to whisper in the little girl's ear, "Go get in the circle, sissy; they'll let you play. Go on." Laurel looked up quickly, a shy, questioning smile on her face, then she moved toward the circle of happy youngsters. No one seemed to pay particular attention when quiet Laurel parted a pair of hands and took them into her own, and Amanda's.

Satisfied for Laurel, Willow moved on. Group games filled the morning hours. Playing them wasn't the same as doing something with one or two special friends, but it was fun, especially the sack race and the shoe-kicking contest. Willow felt bad when she kicked her shoe farther than Miss Barnes', winning that contest. She would be obliged to Miss Barnes for a long time for chasing those mongrel dogs off with her ringing bell.

Waddling Mrs. Butterfield, whose place adjoined The Ranch on the west, won the bermuda onion eating contest. Watching the onion juice running down Mrs. Butterfield's several plump chins, Willow wasn't surprised. Anybody who drank soured milk by the quart as a cure for her dropsy, as Willow had heard Mrs. Butterfield did, ought to be able to eat anything.

When the sweltering sun was noon-high overhead, Willow saw thankfully that women were starting to cover the plank and sawhorse tables with cloths. An almost endless mouth-watering line of food came out from many baskets and boxes and was placed on the tables: crisp fried chicken, enormous platters of pink, sliced ham, fragrant loaves of yeasty brown bread, bowls of early red and white radishes and green onions, steaming pots of baked beans, plus pickles and preserves of every color and description. Jessamyn had done herself proud baking a large pan of cinnamon rolls, and Willow nodded at her with an approving grin when Jessamyn unhesitatingly placed them alongside the luscious cakes and pies from the Baxter Bakery.

Everywhere, young and old were fast losing interest in their games and were coming together to stand in clumps nearer the food-laden tables. Behind

Willow, someone gave a snorting laugh and slapped her palms together. Willow turned and saw Auberta Steele, their leather-faced spinster neighbor. Auberta's brown calloused hands made a whispering as she continued to rub them together. "Working in my west field and smelt this good food clean over there. Free dinner, I told myself. And here I am! Didn't take time to change clothes," the spinster said needlessly. She threw out a board-flat chest to show that she wore a smudged, faded print dress over men's striped suit trousers, she kicked a foot to show heavy work shoes.

Willow frowned. For reasons she wasn't sure about, she didn't care for Auberta Steele. She couldn't fault the spinster's farming ways, though. Miss Steele had the handsomest farm in the county, maybe in the state. Since the south boundary of Auberta's land lay just across the main road from The Ranch, Willow was reminded of that fact, often.

Wanting to forget Auberta Steele, Willow decided maybe she could make herself useful. She was half-starved, if she helped it might hurry things along. A last-minute, huge potato salad was being put together at one of the tables, she saw. Willow hurried over and elbowed into the group. She grabbed up a spare paring knife and set to work peeling boiled potatoes.

Feeling happy and useful, Willow was reaching for her third potato to peel when she heard a sniffing sound just above her left ear. Willow glanced up to see Mrs. Lewis's long nose twitching above her like a rabbit's in a carrot patch. Melinda Kay's mother, though, didn't look like a carrot-happy rabbit, she looked furious. For a few seconds Willow stared, bewildered, at the woman in her ruffles and furbelows, her hairdo so perfect it looked like swoops of chocolate icing. "What—? Me?" she stammered.

"Oh!" she gasped, suddenly remembering how she must smell, how she looked, from her set-to with the mangy dogs. "I—I'm sorry." Willow dropped the knife and the potato and backed off.

Willow had backed several paces but she heard Mrs. Lewis's loud whisper, "Throw that potato away! Peeuw, don't *they* know what soap is?"

Blood pounded at Willow's temples and her face felt blazing hot. *She* was clean. It was the dogs. She turned her back to the tables and took a few more stumbling steps when she heard a second woman volunteer, "Both that girl's folks is foreigners from across the water, one from one country, the other from some place else, don't know where. Got accents so thick I doubt they can understand one another."

Willow halted, feeling sick inside, wanting to run except that her legs felt like heavy wood. Her hands lifted of their own accord toward her ears, as Mrs. Lewis took over the conversation again. "Shiftless, lazy, and good-for-nothing. All these tenant farm families, *just transients*, foreigners and otherwise. Here today, gone tomorrow." From Mrs. Lewis's voice it was clear she believed tenant farmers a blight of the human race.

It's not true, you're wrong, Mrs. Lewis! Willow wanted to shout, but she held her tongue and fought tears stinging her eyes. Because a family moved around a lot didn't necessarily mean they were too lazy and good-for-nothing to settle down. But many people born and raised in one spot seemed to think that. She knew most movers would near give their souls for a place to call their own.

Willow walked around to the far side of an elm tree and shoved her slim back hard against the scratchy bark, not minding the hurt, afraid of the ugly scene she might cause in another minute. Some tenant farm families probably were shiftless and maybe even liked the adventure of always being on the move. Lazy, too. She'd seen some of those whittle and spit kind, who spent more time on their porches than in their fields.

Not all were like that, though. Many tenant farm folk the Fabers had met were nice, clean, hardworking people. Like Mama and Papa. She knew first-hand and with all her heart that they were like that. But Melinda's mother's notion lumped all tenant farm families together like so many rough, scaly potatoes. It wasn't fair!

Besides, maybe it was people like Mrs. Lewis

and her friend, not willing and fair enough to give movers a chance, that forced those same folk to always be ne'er-do-wells. Why should being a newcomer, somebody unpermanent, be something to be ashamed of, anyway? Like they made her feel? Maybe that had something to do with whatever caused some folks to believe they had no chance to better themselves. With her right heel, Willow struck the tree in a fierce kick. They wouldn't do that to her—to her family, no sir!

"Now, don't you worry, Miz Lewis," Willow overheard Auberta Steele say, loud and sudden, "I got my eye on that place they're on, it's just 'cross the road from my south line. A good piece a' property, a nice chunk to add to my place. I've been thinking serious about buying it from the Abraham boys. You'll have no cause to worry about those Fabers, then, they'll be off it."

If lightning had struck the tree Willow leaned against, she couldn't have felt a stronger jolt. She gasped aloud, then sagged against the rough bark of the elm. Her hand went up to cover her mouth. Their place? The Ranch? Auberta Steele? What could Auberta Steele be talking about, she couldn't have their Ranch. It couldn't be. Maybe she didn't hear right.

It was useless to try to convince herself otherwise. She had heard what she had heard. Willow turned suddenly cold; she shivered in the midday sunshine. What were they going to do? She had to tell Papa. . . .

Willow stepped away from the tree. In a worried trance she began to circle around the elm, hands on her hips. They better get to the Abrahams right away, she decided. She and Papa had to let the Abrahams know the Fabers' plans to earn a down payment to put on The Ranch. She had to get Papa to ask Eliot and Egbert Abraham for first chance to buy The Ranch. The Abraham twins were pretty old, and maybe a bit jangled in the upper story, but they were good-hearted, honest. And they were clear-minded enough to understand and were fair enough in their dealings that they'd give her and Papa a decent chance. She was sure of it. Willow breathed deep, looked up satisfied. She had a plan, at least.

Willow stopped pacing and looked toward the bustling, gabbling women at the picnic tables. "I'll show you all," she vowed in a whisper, "even if I have to kill myself with work. The Ranch is going to belong to the Faber family."

"What'd you say?"

Willow whirled, her face turning hot. Conroy Gill stood behind her, his muddy-tan face showing a white-toothed grin. "N-nothing," she answered, and tried to walk around him.

He stepped in her path. "Want to go canoeing with me?"

"Oh, yes, I would . . ." Willow moved closer

to him, then stopped. "No." She shook her head and stumbled back. "I better not. I forgot—"

"How come? You think I'd tip the canoe over or something?" He flexed the muscles in his left arm. "Have no fear."

"No, I know it would be all right, but . . ." Because of her disappointment and apology to him, a lopsided grin was the best Willow could muster. How did you tell a boy that you smelled doggy and wouldn't be good company because of it? Willow shrugged. "Some other time, Conroy, please? And, listen—thanks." She moved away abruptly. She could feel him staring after her, but when she turned to look later, Conroy was at the tables heaping a plate with food. A tiny ache opened inside her. A chance had come, it might have been nice; she'd wanted to go, so much.

Willow's own stomach was growling from emptiness, but she wouldn't go near the tables again, she decided. Someone might get hot under the collar about how she smelled, and looked, and spoiled their appetite. She wished she had gone back home to change and come late to the picnic. It was dumb to worry about it now. She'd just mosey about till it was time to go—and stay away from people as best she could.

Finally, the auction was begun. Miss Barnes, looking young and pretty in a gray and pink print dress, stood on one of the tables to act as auctioneer. People grouped about; the bidding was brisk, with much laughing and good-natured yelling. Almost as soon as it had begun, the auction was over; seven dollars was the top bid for Chandler.

Watching from the sidelines, Willow felt a surge of pleasure and grinned to herself. Mean Old Chandler, Mama's goose, had raised seven dollars to help the Red Cross! As Mama would say, *"Bien, bien!"* It was something to be proud of, a good thing.

The farmer who'd bought Chandler and who held him in a sack between his feet counted the bills into Miss Barnes's hand and Miss Barnes in turn handed the money over to the waiting Mrs. Lewis. Mrs. Lewis! *Her?* Quivering with indignation, Willow remembered then that Mrs. Lewis was president of the local Red Cross chapter; Melinda had said so in class.

Willow could hold back no longer. Straight as an arrow she made her brisk way through the crowd that was breaking up. Directly in front of Mrs. Lewis she halted. Lifting her chin and looking the austere Mrs. Lewis full in the face, Willow said, "The goose came from our farm. My mama and papa donated it, to do their part. I thought you'd want to know."

Mrs. Lewis blinked, her mouth sagged open, then snapped shut. She looked down at the money in her hand as though uncertain what to do with it, then stuffed it into her shiny black handbag. Without a word to Willow, she turned and walked away.

Willow watched her go, swallowing something

that came up in her throat. It probably hadn't done one bit of good, telling Mrs. Lewis, but *she* felt a lot better. Willow lifted her chin. Now, she had to get home and talk to Papa.

four

WILLOW made her way swiftly through the picnic grove calling to a brother or sister when she could spot them. "We've got a three-mile walk and chores when we get home," she reminded them when they were all together. "Let's go."

"I had fun! Did you?" Laurel piped as she took Willow's hand. Willow smiled but didn't answer.

"They ate all my cinnamon rolls." Jessamyn glowed, waving an empty pan. "Farley Baxter said they were better even than his Pa's bakery rolls."

Seeing Jessy's flushed face and glowing blue eyes, Willow thought, *And you're a lot prettier than his Pa, too. Maybe that had something to do with it.* But she didn't say it aloud.

"Me an' Adan was on the winning baseball team," Walsh announced in a proud boast.

" 'Adan and I *were*'," Willow corrected.

"You was playin' ball?" Adan asked Willow, puffing with his lower lip to blow his hair out of his eyes. "I didn't see you. Which team? I sure didn't see you anywhere."

"Yeah, where were you, Willow?" Walsh asked, wiping his dirty face with a still grimier sleeve.

Sighing, Willow looked at her brothers for a long moment. No need to spoil their good mood with her troubles, she decided. She shrugged. "I was around." She motioned for the others to follow and swung into an easy lope across the railroad tracks in the direction of the train depot, the sky-reaching grain warehouses, and further along, home.

On the benches by the depot, when they reached it, Willow noted returning soldiers sitting like crows on a fence. There was little work for them, she'd heard; others had their jobs now. The men looked so useless. It was sad.

At the next corner they turned east. Here, tidy little houses and wispy alder trees lined the brick streets. The tantalizing odor of frying potatoes and meat came from one of the homes, causing Willow's stomach to grind painfully. She hurried faster.

The houses thinned out. As they left Seena behind, Willow and the others could see Auberta Steele's farm ahead of them. In past times whenever Papa could spare her, Willow remembered, she had loved to take Eagle out for a run and at the same time explore the countryside where they lived at the time. It had truly pleasured her, seeing some of the beautiful homes and farms, imagining what it would be like living there.

You couldn't possibly look at Auberta's farm and not admire it, no matter what you thought of the owner, Willow thought, now. Smooth stone walls fenced the front of the farmstead. Beautiful elm trees flanked either side of the long lane to the tall, green-shuttered, white house. The red barns and sheds had a well-kept, but industrious look. A weed wouldn't dast try to grow in any of Auberta's wide fields, Willow figured.

The Fabers turned south and continued for a quarter of a mile, reached the main road, then turned east again toward The Ranch. Walsh suddenly whooped, "Looka there! Look at that fella running—what's he so cottonpickin' scared of?"

Willow looked where Walsh pointed and saw a man on Auberta Steele's land, racing through the oatfield as though the coals of hell were burning his heels. Willow shaded her eyes for a better look and caught sight of the tall, oddly attired woman with fists in the air, following the man in loping strides. "It's Auberta Steele," Willow mumbled, "running off another hired man for making some blunder or other."

"Look at him go!" Walsh cackled, dancing in the dust of the road.

"I bet she beat him up once a'ready," Adan guessed, grinning.

"It's sure a silly way for a woman with her money to act." Jessamyn sniffed. "If I had everything she does, I'd never act so weird."

"He did something wrong, you can be sure of

that. Old spinster Steele doesn't allow mistakes on her place." She admitted grudgingly, "That's why her farm is as good as it is. Papa says if Auberta's help does wrong to her land or her animals in any way, she runs him off quick as scat; he's finished. But neither of them is doing those oats any good today."

Walsh was still dancing and chuckling, punching the hot late afternoon air with quick jabs of his chubby fists. Willow grinned in spite of herself. "Walsh, stop it," she chided. "We got to get home." She felt heartened by the sight of Auberta Steele chasing off another hired man. How could the spinster take on the work of more land if she was most of the time shorthanded?

After supper, when she and Papa were alone in the barn seeing that the animals were bedded for the night, Willow told Papa what she had overheard at the picnic. She repeated what Auberta Steele had said about planning to buy The Ranch, but left out the remarks about the family being shiftless. For nothing in the world would she pass on to Papa and Mama the other details of her miserable day—the hurtful remarks made by the good ladies of Seena.

"We ought to see the Abrahams right away, shouldn't we, Papa?" The urgency she was feeling was in Willow's voice, making it a tone higher.

Papa frowned. "Ay have to cultivate corn,

potatoes, all this week, weeds come up fast." He looked down as Jingles came into the barn; smilingly, the brown dog leaned against Papa's legs to be petted.

"Papa, this is very important," Willow reminded, joining him in petting Jingles.

He nodded and stroked his moustache as he straightened. "*Yah*, is important. You right about some tings, daughter. Is good time to buy farm. Ay know changes we could make if place ours. We get better crops, more profit." An earnest look came into Papa's face. "Someday it be a debt-free farm, God willing. I like that, *yah*. Better day, then, for whole family. I want to care for you all, good."

"Then we go to see Egbert and Eliot Abraham tomorrow, Papa?" Willow pressed, "tomorrow?"

Papa's face crinkled into a smile. He patted Willow's shoulder and nodded.

A great weight lifted from Willow's mind. Papa always made good a promise.

Next morning, Mama thrust a fragrant towel-covered dish at Willow when they were ready to go. "Take mulberry pie," Mama told her, "and bowl of cottage cheese I make fresh." She motioned for a sleepy, nightgowned Jessamyn to go for the cottage cheese.

"In a minute, in a minute," Jessy mumbled, rubbing her face pink as she tried to come awake. She staggered toward the door to go out to the deep, cold well where the milk and cheese were kept.

"Hurry, sleepyhead," Willow ordered good-naturedly. "This will all help put the Abrahams in a better mood when we talk to them."

"*Non!*" Mama scolded Willow. "Bribe old gentlemen, no. Good neighbors, that's all." She gave Willow a gentle swat. "Go with your Papa and be most nice *mademoiselle*."

The reminder to behave herself did not faze Willow's high spirits. Moments later, settling their mounts into an easy trot, she and Papa followed the dusty road toward the Abraham's place—Papa on his bay Dulcie, of course; Willow riding Eagle. With a small sigh of pleasure, Willow reached forward to stroke Eagle's dazzling white shoulder. In the early morning sunshine, head lifted, Eagle was so beautiful!

But then, everything looked fine this morning, Willow decided. The wild daisies and tall roadside grasses were quivery with chirruping wrens and sparrows. Tilting her head, Willow took in the enormous expanse of deep blue sky, where white clouds floated like castles. She and Jessy had often thought clouds looked like castles. She could remember one time, especially. They had been living that year on a rented farm in Pottawatomie County.

EGG-SIZED hail had come like knives to cut to pieces Papa's corn crop and Mama's whole garden. After, it was one of the times there wasn't enough to eat; they'd come close to starving. Sitting side by side on the splintery step of the falling down porch of that old house, sucking in their empty stomachs so they wouldn't hurt as much, eight-year-old Willow and Jessy had put their arms around one another and set to dreaming.

The castle in the cloud they watched was plain as anything. And they were the grand lovely ladies in velvet gowns who lived in the castle. They wore their hair in masses of shiny curls, and many rings glittered on their fingers. The best part came when they went to dinner in the castle. Long tables with white cloths were loaded with dishes of delicious food. In the middle of one table was a golden brown pig sizzling on an enormous platter, a red apple stuck in its mouth. Jessy begged to have the apple; Willow was glad to take the roast pork.

WILLOW shook her head to clear it of the memory that could even now hurt a little. That time was behind them. They would never have to go back there. Now that she thought about it, she remembered the farm owner coming and asking them to leave, to get off that rented farm. As though Papa brought the hail storm, ruining the chance for profit for himself and the owner that year!

Willow was glad to see that they were reaching the end of their five-mile journey south to the Abrahams. She stole a look at Papa. There was a lot she didn't know about him, probably. She ought to take the time to think about him, his side of things.

The Abraham brothers' farmhouse must have been one of the grandest in these parts in bygone

days, Willow decided, as they approached. Ginger-
bread trim decorated the many eaves and porches of
the old sprawling two-story house. The house may
have been white once, but it was now a weathered
gray.

Willow's heart beat faster in anticipation as
she and Papa tied their horses at the front gate and
took the stone path through a tangle of roses and
honeysuckle vine to the wide front porch. Papa
knocked on the door, waited, then knocked again.
He rubbed his hickory brown knuckles after a bit
and pounded the door some more. Willow hoped he
wouldn't give up and want to return home without
seeing the Abrahams.

"You know they're likely at home, Papa," Willow said, "but living in that one room down in the
cellar like they do makes it hard for them to hear
all the way up through this big house." She waited
patiently beside Papa. At long last, a shuffling sound
came from the other side of the door. Willow put
a wide smile on as the door creaked open just a
crack. A faded blue eye under a thick mane of
silvery hair blinked at them.

Willow craned her neck to see if the old face
carried a walrus moustache. None. "It's Egbert," she
whispered out of the corner of her mouth to Papa.
The lean twin, Eliot, was the one who sported the
handsome moustache. Egbert's little round face was
clean-shaven.

"Good morning, Mr. Abraham," Papa spoke,

"is Karl Faber and daughter, Willow Sabrina. We talk to you, *yah?*"

The door swung open, and Egbert's withered lips formed a beaming smile. "Friends," he cackled, "come in." His knotted hand beckoned them inside. "You come to visit at a good time—Ellamae had her kittens just last night," he told them proudly. "Come see them."

"We came to—" Willow began. She stopped when she caught the shake of Papa's head, the look of amused patience in his pale blue eyes. She grinned back at Papa, then said, "I'd love to see the kittens, Mr. Abraham. Here's a mulberry pie and fresh cottage cheese Mama sent you." She held them out for him to see. "I'll carry them for you."

Egbert's old eyes lit up, his chin shook just a little. "Pie?" he quavered, "and cottage cheese? It's been a long time. . . . Thank you, thank you." He cleared his throat. "Follow me, follow me," he urged.

Even though it wasn't their first visit, Willow was glad for another chance to see the interesting old house. They followed the round-shouldered figure through numerous rooms and halls, their footsteps causing small puffs of silvery dust to rise from the rose-colored carpet. As before, a hodgepodge of books, clothes, dishes, and tools lay in haphazard piles on fine wood furniture—all coated with dust.

On the walls, papered in a gold stripe that was stained and peeling, hung walnut-framed portraits of earlier Abrahams. Willow tripped suddenly,

looked down and saw a saddle on the floor behind
an elegant satin-upholstered settee. That wasn't there,
last time!

They came to a door opening to narrow cellar
stairs and Egbert led the way down, taking the stairs
one at a time with aching slowness. "Eliot," he
called chortling, "these folks want to see Ellamae's
kittens." He looked back at Willow and Papa, then
pointed in disgust at a brown spot on the step. "Eliot
chews," he told them in terrible embarrassment.
"Nasty. Nasty tobacco."

They reached the bottom of the stairs, and
Egbert opened a door that led into the single room
where the Abraham twins ate, slept, and entertained
company. Willow gave a tiny gasp and breathed
out as much as she was able. The stench of burned
oatmeal was awful.

From a worn black leather couch with horse-
hair popping through the holes in it, Egbert's twin,
Eliot, got to his feet to greet them. Behind his walrus
moustache a big smile warmed his gaunt cheeks. His
layers of mismatched clothes, Willow thought, made
Eliot look like a thin, flat ragdoll, somehow. But
his hand, when it caught hers after Papa's, was warm
and strong.

"Welcome," Eliot said. "Ellamae was hoping
for company so she could show off her new little
babies." With his shoulders leading more eagerly
than the rest of his body could follow, Eliot took
them across the room to a huge iron stove. He

pointed a finger that wouldn't stay still. Behind the stove, curled on a pair of long-handled underwear, was gray-striped Ellamae and her sleeping children—one black fuzzball, one yellow, and one striped like herself.

"They're the cutest kittens I've ever seen," Willow told the old men in a whisper, meaning it.

"*Yah*," Papa agreed, smiling, "they beautiful kittens."

Fifteen minutes or so later, they sat about the round oak table in the center of the room, drinking weak, terrible-tasting coffee and eating large slices of Mama's mulberry pie. "We come with business," Papa said at last. "Mr. Eliot, Mr. Egbert—my wife, my daughter, and me, we would like to buy your farm we renting now. . . ."

Willow waited anxiously for the elderly twins to say something. She spooned a last bite of juicy black berries into her mouth and held the fruit there a moment, tasting, finding it hard to swallow. In the next second her hopes, all their plans could crumble. Willow's scalp tightened painfully at the base of her skull; she swallowed hard and watched the Abrahams as one crinkling pair of watery eyes looked into the other.

She thought she made out a look of agreement between the old men, but which *way* they agreed, Willow couldn't guess. Eliot spoke for them. "It would help us, if you took the stagecoach place off our hands," he said. Willow sighed in sudden deep relief. "Everything is too much," Eliot continued. "This house is too big for us two old men to keep up. We have too much land to worry about."

Egbert's head bobbed. "All Eliot and me need our last years is this room, our automobile, our cow, and our handful of chickens. I have to do all the chores," he added, with a pointed look at his twin.

Eliot, scraping his plate for the last bite of berry juice, didn't see. "Let's talk about it," he said, lifting his spoon jerkily toward his eager mouth. "Maybe you can stay right where you are and raise your nice big family, Karl."

Willow leaned forward to listen carefully, but a dizzy happiness had enveloped her and she found it hard to follow the complicated plans the Abrahams and her father laid out. She did understand that the price for The Ranch would be thirty-five dollars an acre, and Papa must raise five hundred dollars cash as down payment. That would be awful hard to do! Usually, one-third of the money they profited from their crops was only about three-hundred dollars. This was paid out as rent. All the rest of their profit went to pay bills for seed, tools, and family needs. They'd need two-hundred dollars more than they'd ever earned before.

Withdrawn into her worry, Willow was only partly aware of talk about a lawyer to draw up papers as soon as Papa got the down payment. Then she heard something that cheered her. For two years after they made the down payment, Eliot was saying, they would not have to pay on the principal. Papa would only have to pay the interest. That would give them a breather before they began to make yearly payments on the principal and interest! The gentle old men were fair!

A vision of Auberta Steele's leathery, grinning face flashed into Willow's mind. "Has-has anyone else offered to buy The Ranch, our place, from you?" Willow questioned. She traced the table's edge with a blunt thumbnail.

The twins threw quizzical looks at one another and shook their heads. "The shape it's been in for years, who would want it?" Eliot answered her. "We had a strange mixture of tenants until you came along, Faber. A few of them were ambitious, but they were hard on the land, grinding all they could get out of it for the short time they leased it. Still others were lazy, wouldn't work, and let everything go. A few cheated us. One good man, like you, moved away after his wife died. Is that human nature, all?" Eliot nodded *yes* to his own remarks.

Mrs. Lewis, Willow thought fleetingly, who believed all tenants were the same, lazy, could learn from Eliot Abraham. But, there was something more important than that, and she had to be sure, "You'll remember that Papa wants first chance to buy The Ranch? You won't forget?"

Egbert smiled impatiently, he seemed to have something important on his mind that she wasn't aware of. "Yes, yes, you have our word. We won't forget. Hark!" he said suddenly, and cupped a gnarled hand behind his ear. Willow saw the old men exchange a happy, knowing look.

She listened and heard the tiny mewing sounds from in back of the stove. "Are we upsetting the kittens? They're awful new and tiny. Maybe we should go?" She stood up. Papa followed suit and shook hands firmly with the elderly, beaming twins.

Eliot escorted them this time, up through the dusty, cluttered house. If there'd be a little time from work on The Ranch one day, Willow mused, she'd like to come back and really explore the Abraham's house, if they wouldn't mind. It'd be almost as good as a history lesson. And, a small secret part of her had always felt something special for old beautiful houses like this one.

As she and Papa went out the front door, Egbert called softly after them, "Come back and see the kittens when their eyes are open."

Willow smiled over her shoulder and nodded. "We'll be back."

five

EARLY in the morning, a week after Willow and her father had visited the Abrahams, Papa hitched Ben their mule to the cultivator and attacked the weeds coming up fast in the south forty cornfield, having finished the northeast field. Willow followed with her hoe to catch the weeds the cultivator missed, working without complaint because it was a move toward making their big dream come true.

That afternoon, a chugging auto came gradually into hearing and coughed to a stop at the far, roadside edge of their field. Willow rested the hoe in the crook of her arm as she shaded her eyes to look and with her other small fist she rubbed at the pain in her back. Her perspiring forehead wrinkled in worry. What had brought Egbert Abraham to see them so soon? He and Eliot wouldn't be changing their minds, would they? They couldn't, not now! Had Auberta Steele been to see them? Willow drew in long, shuddering breaths, and waited.

Like a bouncy little boy, the old man clambered from the Abrahams' dusty black 1917 Model T touring car and waved at her. "Papa, a visitor," Willow called.

Papa had seen Egbert for himself and was anchoring the cultivator to a stop. He wrapped Ben's reins about the handles, and then trudged down the row toward the old man, taking out a faded red bandanna to mop his face. Willow fell in behind with her hoe slung over her shoulder. In the clatter coming from Egbert, she thought she heard the words, "good news" and her curiosity climbed.

Egbert's pudding-like body was actually bouncing. "Our grandnephew, Frank Tucker, has come to make his home with me and Eliot," he yelped happily as they came within earshot. "He is fifteen years old, our niece, Jenny's boy, from Missoura." He sobered a trifle. "She passed on a few weeks ago. We're his only kin."

Willow made a sympathetic noise, still wondering what this was all about, and if this was all Egbert had come to tell them.

After a moment, Papa said, "We sorry to hear that, about niece. But is good about boy. He help, be company for you and your brother, *yah?*" As though he couldn't wait to say it, Papa changed the subject with a wave of his arm that took in their fields, "What you think of place? See wheat over there? Like thick lovely grass, *yah?* Small field, maybe, but we get fifteen, twenty bushel to acre, I think. Pretty good for spring wheat."

Willow looked, too, and felt a warm glow, herself.

Egbert blinked in the bright sunlight, and smiled. "You're a good farmer, Karl Faber. Eliot and me, we don't question that. We're glad to have you on this place."

Inside Willow, a knot of worry loosened. "Where's Eliot today?" she asked. "Is he at home with your nephew?"

"Eliot doesn't feel too good," Egbert said with a shake of his head. "We bought oranges while we were in town to get Frank, oranges that came all the way from California. Eliot ate three of them before I could make him stop. He's waiting for me in the car, with Frank." Egbert motioned toward the empty automobile parked on the road's edge. "Over there."

The hot sun had got to her, or to Egbert, for certain. Willow looked quizzically at the empty automobile parked a few yards away. "Mr. Abraham, there's nobody in your auto."

"Of course there—" Egbert turned to see for himself. The old man's mouth fell open before he covered it with a wrinkled hand. Right before Willow's eyes he seemed to shrink inside his suit. His stiff collar came up around his ears. "My stars, my stars, my stars!" he exclaimed.

"They fall out?" Papa asked, aghast.

"They just—disappeared?" Willow hurried to the old man's side.

He looked scared, then began to giggle in nervous agitation. "We were having soup at Willert's Restaurant, by Evans's Boarding House on Main Street. You know where that is? Young Frank waited for us to pick him up there, after he got off the train. *I came off without them*, yes indeedy, I was in such a hurry to tell the good news, I forgot to bring them along. That's what I did."

Papa and Willow said nothing, but the silence that followed was filled with questions. Egbert had actually left his own twin brother in town, forgetting him? And the nephew he was so excited about? Standing on a street corner, somewhere, maybe? Waiting? From the corner of her eye, Willow caught the twitching of Papa's gray-gold moustache that told her he was struggling not to laugh. She had to clamp her own jaws tight. She looked at the ground, pinned her attention on a black bug that was scuttling around and over the clods of fresh-turned earth.

Looking quite a bit like the bug, Egbert scuttled back to his automobile where he yanked the crank up. "I hope, I hope, Eliot had a second bowl of soup, not another orange," he cried, just before he cranked again and the engine sputtered and choked to life. A huge cloud of dust settled over Willow and Papa as the Model T whipped about in the road and headed with a popping roar in the opposite direction, back the way it had come. The auto horn could be heard *oogah-ing* most of the way into Seena.

Willow wiped the dust from her face on her sleeve, and her feeling of laughter went with it. She followed Papa up the row, frowning. "The Abrahams are awful mixed-up sometimes," she said to the back of Papa's sweat-darkened blue shirt. "You don't think they'll forget the promise they made us?"

"Ay don't worry too much about old gentlemen a little vacant in upper story," Papa answered. "They remember, I think. They give us word." He snorted. "Ay worry more about sunflower in cornfield. Got to get it out now, soon it comes up. Sunflower be the devil to chop out if stalks get big, woody."

"I know, Papa, I know." Willow sighed, feeling a little better, at least about the Abrahams. "The morning glory weed is about as bad as the sunflower. How come the weeds have to grow faster than the crops?" She didn't really expect an answer, and Papa gave none. She slashed with her hoe, stopping now and then to tamp back in a tender green corn plant Papa's cultivator, or Ben's hoof, had knocked down.

Willow worked on, chopping, chopping, at the weeds. Her thoughts turned to Frank Tucker. What would he be like, this boy who had come to live with his old uncles? What would he think of them? Would he be nice? With more caution, Willow's thoughts edged into another subject, still new enough to her to give her a jittery, airy feeling inside. This year, this school, would she have a beau? How about

—maybe—this Frank Tucker? Suddenly annoyed with herself, Willow grunted aloud. For all she knew, Frank Tucker was ugly as a toad and ignorant as a salamander. For heaven's sake!

Besides, she decided, with a shadow of misgiving, with all the work to do on The Ranch, there'd be precious little time for such as *that*.

Springtime's steamy days ended, and June's searing winds arrived. Crops shot up, visibly higher each living day. Willow worried that the hot winds would sap the life right out of the corn, but it flourished and would be more than "knee-high by the Fourth of July." She turned more and more of her barn chores over to Walsh and Adan so she could help Papa keep the fields clean of weeds; all too soon the corn would be too high to take the cultivator into the field.

Weeks passed, and still Willow hadn't met Frank Tucker, the Abraham's fifteen-year-old nephew. But Jessy had seen him, close up, in town, and from her description he was no toad. Once or twice, Willow's curiosity had nearly gotten the best of her, and she'd been tempted to go riding over near the Abrahams'. She could ask for a real tour of that wonderful old house, that'd be an excuse. Getting acquainted wouldn't be any trouble. . . .

But, there just wasn't time yet. The cultivating was hardly finished before it was time to put up their large field of prairie hay. Next year, Papa vowed, he was going to plant this field to alfalfa. The days were long. Pitching the windrowed, sweet-smelling hay for hours at a time left Willow too tired, too sore in every muscle, to think seriously of going visiting. When you had a dream as important as buying The Ranch, it had to come first, Willow reminded herself time and again.

On the last day of haying, the family was at noon dinner in the stifling kitchen when Papa announced that he would be going to town next morning. "Two pigs ready for market." He looked proud as he stroked his moustache; his eyes were as shiny bright as his perspiring skin. "They weigh two-hundred pounds apiece, I bet. Willow, if you see to weeds in potato patch tomorrow, Walsh can go to help me. I find out if we can get a threshing crew for our wheat. Maybe a small crew come to our place after they finish big farms."

Willow nodded thoughtfully. She knew the wheat was almost ready to cut and shock—she'd seen Papa take wheat heads from a stalk to chew and feel the break of the kernels in his teeth, then nod. With a look at her mother, Willow asked, "We're going to have a fair potato harvest, too, aren't we?"

Mama put down her fork carefully. Her work-weary face softened with a smile. "*Bien.*" She reached up and deftly tucked the graying tendril into the neat bun of hair at the back of her head. "And Jessy, she has fourteen pounds of butter now to sell, and eggs. You take tomorrow, eh, Karl?"

"*Yah,* I sell the pigs, butter, and eggs tomorrow.

Sell some of your fryer-chickens, too, if you want, Julie." Papa gave his younger children a stern look. "You pick bugs off potato plants while I go," he said. "Bugs so bad we get no potatoes if we not careful. Hear your Papa?"

Adan had heard. His thin, summer-begrimed face got an unhappy look that in turn showed in Laurel's and Clay's faces. But the three of them answered in mournful unison, "Mmm-hmm, Papa."

Papa had always expected his children to work, Willow was thinking, but Adan, especially, tried to get out of it. He didn't seem to be lazy particularly, it was more that he found other things, his own things, far more interesting—and to him, more important.

With little effort, Willow could guess that what Adan would really like to do tomorrow was be off to some creek to fish for sun perch and bullheads or swim in his birthday suit. Or, do whatever he was up to in the grove for hours and hours at a time. Too bad. Adan would have to learn about hard work the same as the rest of them. "Don't worry, Papa, I'll be right there in the patch to see that all of them work," Willow said.

"If we get all the bugs picked off the potato plants," Laurel said, threading a finger anxiously around a wisp of her hair, "then can we play in the grove?"

Willow noted that her little sister's face was not so peaked as it used to be—she was a healthy tan this summer. Braver, too, to ask a special favor after Papa'd laid down the law. But Laurel wasn't through. The little girl picked at a button on the chest of her faded green dress. "Adan says there's gold treasure buried under them trees in the grove. We been digging and digging for it," she said, excitement in her voice.

"Gold?" It was all Willow could do to keep from laughing at Adan, Laurel, and Clay across the table from her. "Listen, you three, there isn't any *gold*, and all of us got to work hard."

Mama voiced her own opinion. "*Non, non,* you get dirty playing in dirt. Is waste of soap, wash your clothes all time."

Jessamyn, tearing a slice of bread in two dainty pieces, spoke up, "Like Willow says, there isn't any treasure buried in the grove, but some nine-year-old dumbbell"—she looked at Adan—"with a crazy wild imagination, thinks that there is."

Adan purpled; he smacked a fist on the table, just missing his plate of half-eaten food. "There is too gold buried in the grove," he blurted, "and I'm agonna find it. When I do I am buying me a Daisy Air Rifle, some checkers, too, and probably a great big drum!" He looked as if he might have said more, but it was plain he was close to crying and didn't want the tears to come.

"If you'd keep your nose out of the Sears and Roebuck catalogue, you'd be more help around here,

Adan," Willow said. Going through the "wishbook" was Adan's full-time indoor occupation.

"No more argue today," Mama warned. "Save yourselves for work must be done."

Willow nodded in agreement and leaned back in her chair for another minute or two of rest. She watched silently as Adan guarded his face with one hand so Mama and Papa couldn't see him and thumbed his nose at her with his other. Willow stared back at him with casual unconcern, knowing that would spite him more than if she raised a fuss.

Next morning right after breakfast, Papa sat high on the wagon seat ready to go, their baskets of eggs and crocks of butter nestled in straw in the wagon bed behind him. Walsh was close by, carrying an old cane with which to prod the two snuffling, grunting pigs along the road to Seena.

"Try to haggle, Papa, Walsh," Willow called, following the creaking wagon and Walsh guiding his grunting pigs, out to the road. "We're going to need all the extra cash we can get." She didn't wait to see them out of sight, but hurried back into the kitchen where she poured coal oil into three empty lard buckets. Adan, Laurel, and little Clay could carry the buckets with them down the potato rows, to drop the bugs into the coal oil and destroy them.

Willow set the young ones to work picking bugs off the still dew-wet, deep green potato plants. She then took up her hoe, thinking that the tool was in her hands so much this summer it was becoming like a part of her body. Willow worked in silence for a time, paying small heed to the young ones' chatter. She began to hum to herself, then sang softly,

"Oh, the moon shines tonight on pretty Redwing,
The breeze is sighing, the nightbirds crying . . .

The morning hours passed slowly, and Willow found few reasons to scold the bug pickers who worked along steadily enough.

"Drat," Willow whispered suddenly. She left the hoe to mark the spot where she must take up the weeding again and headed for the outhouse.

"Where you takin' off to?" Adan demanded.

"You get three guesses," Willow tossed over her shoulder, and kept going.

When Willow stepped out of the small building, she glanced toward the potato patch and stopped short. The dazzling sun glanced off three abandoned buckets. Now where had they gone off to? Maybe, she reasoned, they had gone to the house for a drink of water, or a slice of Mama's fresh-baked bread she could smell all the way out here. They'd be back, shortly.

A tiny seed of anger started to grow in Willow when a long spell passed and the youngsters didn't return to the patch. "Lazy little scalawags," she

muttered aloud. What was wrong with them, anyway? They wanted to stay on The Ranch as much
as she did; they'd claimed to loud enough when they
agreed to try to buy the place—all of them working
hard to do it. Did they think they could quit this
soon?

And how could she get anything done if she
had to keep after them all the time? She had a good
idea where they'd be—that grove! She'd put them
back to work so fast it would make their heads swim!
Willow wiped her sweaty face on a sleeve, left her
hoe one more time, and with angry, long-legged
strides headed for the cottonwood grove in back of
the old house.

Adan was the cause; Laurel and four-year-old
Clay would do whatever he put into their heads.
When she was nine, Adan's age, she was putting in
near a full day's work alongside Papa. Walsh had,
too, last year. It was time Adan was taught a lesson.

It was a degree or two cooler in the shade of
the grove. For an instant, Willow felt a flash of
sympathy toward her younger brothers and little
sister, but it was quickly gone. If the whole family
spent their time playing, keeping cool in the shade,
how'd they get The Ranch?

She let the sound of murmuring voices be her
guide. Willow jogged far back into the grove until
she spotted the three of them squatted around a
black hole they were digging at the foot of a giant

old cottonwood tree. A startled look showed her similar holes at the bases of quite a few other trees.

Out of breath from her run, short of patience, Willow gasped, "What—what in the name of Moses do you think you're doing?"

Adan, looking guilty, puffed his hair out of his eyes and went on digging.

Laurel answered, "We're digging for treasure, Willow. Don't be mad . . ." She was squatting, Amanda tight under one arm; a spoon to dig with gripped in her other hand.

Willow drew a long deep breath. Take it easy with them, she cautioned herself, 'cause if they get to sulking too much, what work you do get out of 'em won't be worth a tinker's darn. "There isn't any treasure," she said patiently. "You're just making useless holes in the ground, when you ought to be getting at those potato bugs like Papa said. You're not done. All of you, back to the patch, now." She pointed.

Adan glared at her, wiped his nose with the back of his hand, leaving a moustache of dirt. "Go away."

Willow choked back a sharp retort, but made it plain she was waiting for them.

Clay, the little daredevil one—he'd never been afraid of her or anything else—went right on digging as though he were deaf. It added fuel to Willow's exasperation. She started toward him, wanting to yank him up by the back of his overall suspenders and shake him. Adan rose and barred the way. His chin jutted stubbornly like a bulldog's, his uncombed hair was a tangle that made him look even more ferocious. "Stay away from my little brother," he ground out.

The little smart aleck! Willow gave a half-laugh. "Don't be dumb, Adan, Clay is my little brother, too." She shook her finger. "And he's not too little to work, picking potato bugs especially. Both of you—you—" at a sudden loss for words, Willow gulped.

Adan took that chance to try a different approach. "Listen, Sis," he said in a confiding, honeyed voice, "I know there is a thousand dollars in gold hidden here. Itchy Irwin's brother, Tony, told me all about it."

Willow shook her head. "No, there—"

"There was this lady, Willow," Laurel interrupted in an excited whisper, "an' she heard this outlaw gang, saw 'em comin', up to her house, see? Long, long time ago, it was. Before the outlaws got in her house, the lady hid her thousand dollars in gold so they wouldn't get it. She gave 'em dinner, an' she went right on a'washin' her clothes while they near tore her house apart lookin' for tne gold. The robbers heard the daddy coming and they got scared and run off with no gold." Laurel's eyes were glowing, she took a second to kiss Amanda. "Know where the lady hid it, Willow? She had the gold in a bag right there in the bottom of her washtub, in the clothes and dirty old washwater, all that time!"

"I heard—" Willow began, but now it was little Clay who jumped to his feet to tell her more.

"When the daddy got home," Clay crowed, "he took 'da bag of gold out of the dirty water and buried it safe. Under a cottonwood tree. Right here. A 'sousand dollars!"

Adan finished the story triumphantly, "Buried money, *gold*, lots of it!"

"Buried money, my foot!" Willow said through clenched jaws. She gave each of the three of them a long, level look. "You've just got part of that story and you haven't even got that part right. The gold was buried on a place 'way west of here, and the man was watched when he buried it. The man who saw him bury the money dug the gold up and left these parts for good. Tell that to Itchy Irwin's brother, Adan, 'cause you are wasting time. Get on back to the potato patch, now, you got work to do and so have I."

She waited for them to follow her lead, but Adan spread his legs wide, planted his feet, and shook his head. "You don't know everything." He glowered at her. "You don't know hardly nothing."

"Please, Willow, don't make us go," Laurel begged, twisting her free hand in the skirt of her ragged dress. "It's hot in that old potato patch, and them bugs is awful nasty."

Clay had squatted back down, his face under his mop of softly curling hair was a picture of unworried calm as he began to dig again in the dirt. Willow's patience snapped. "All of you, move!" she yelled. "Right now!"

Laurel led the way, tears welling in her eyes. Clay toddled after, not seeming to really mind what they did. But Adan, older, threw Willow a scorching look. "Why don't you get a blacksnake whip and beat us?" he snarled. "Yuh mean old witch. Willow-the-whip," he taunted, "Willow-the-whip."

Laurel and Clay picked up the chant. "Willow-the-whip," the three of them spat at her hatefully. "Willow whip. Willow whip."

Willow fought an impulse to cover her ears with her hands and dug her fingers into her hips instead. Her eyes burned and a lump swelled in her throat. She hated to be called names. She was *Willow Sabrina Faber*, that's who! Not "good-for-nothing," the name she'd been called at the picnic, or "Willow-the-whip," as her own brothers and little sister were calling her now. Afraid to trust her voice, Willow silently jabbed an unquestioning finger toward the potato patch, then watched through a blur as the three of them trotted back to it.

Times like this, she hated being the oldest, a big sister. She'd rather be one of *them*.

six

NEXT day, Walsh joined Willow hoeing the potato patch while the younger ones continued, with fading resentment, to pick bugs off the potato plants.

While she hoed, Willow's thoughts were with Papa who was overhauling the big binder, the largest piece of machinery on The Ranch. The wheat was almost ready for cutting and binding, then for a few days' curing period before the threshers came.

Papa was sharpening the sickles, mending the canvas conveyors, and checking the binding and tying mechanisms to make sure they were working right. She knew that a breakdown in the middle of harvest, one that lasted hours or maybe even days, could cause the wheat seed to shatter on the stalk and fall wasted to the ground. They couldn't let that happen!

"Papa remembered to get plenty of binder twine in town yesterday, didn't he?" Willow asked Walsh as she chopped weeds.

"Yup." Walsh rested on his hoe and wiped his shiny red face on his sleeve. "Got the twine. And everything else on Mama's list—coal oil, new lamp wicks, matches, flour, sugar—beans."

"Was there any money left?" Willow wailed. "Didn't any of it go to the nest egg to buy this place?"

"Spent all Mama's butter and egg money," Walsh told her. "But most of the money we got for the pigs, Papa put in the yellow jar."

"I hope to gosh," Willow said, relieved. The yellow crockery jar, hidden high in the kitchen cupboard, was marked to hold their savings for the down payment on The Ranch. "I worry about getting any money for these potatoes," she told Walsh, "don't know how long I can keep the kids helping." She nodded in the direction of Adan, Laurel, and Clay, who were slowing down, lackadaisical, as they picked bugs at the opposite end of the patch.

"Adan is hell-bent certain he's going to find treasure in the grove, and the littler ones ain't got better sense than to do his digging for him," Walsh agreed. He laughed. "So far, ol' Adan's dug up a dead dog's skeleton and a rusty buckle. Some treasure." Walsh snickered to himself, grew silent, snickered again.

"Adan wastes valuable time," Willow grunted, "an' it's so important we all work and earn extra money this year."

Like a sign sent from some unknown source to back up her statement, a large grasshopper made itself evident in Willow's line of vision. It was as though she was suddenly alone with the grasshopper.

Her eyes followed as the insect leaped aimlessly—here, there, over, across; Willow's breath caught. How much like their old way of life was that grasshopper moving on, moving on.

Willow shivered, tried to tear her glance from the grasshopper. Whoever paid any attention to a grasshopper? Nobody did. You crunched him under your foot, not even seeing him most times. A nothing. Willow swallowed a dryness in her throat. People, she thought, are maybe forgotten after they're dead, in time. And that, in a way, was bad. But how awful—much worse to be—be never noticed while you live. Like a grasshopper. N-nothing.

"I know how you could make some money for pretty sure, Willow," Walsh was saying. With some difficulty, still shaken, Willow looked at her brother. He scratched at the grimy railroad tracks of sweat in the creases of his chubby neck.

"How?" she choked out.

From the back pocket of his overalls, Walsh took out a soiled square of folded paper and brought it to Willow. She unfolded the paper and read. "A handbill. About a Fourth of July celebration they're going to have in the Seena Picnic Grove? So what?" She wadded the paper and tossed it back at Walsh. "Wasting time going to fool things like that can't get us any money." Willow moved faster with her hoe, looking carefully to make sure she didn't step on the grasshopper, but it was gone.

"You didn't read that bottom line, I bet." Walsh

threw the wad of paper back at Willow and it landed at her feet in the soft, turned earth.

"What line?" she asked suspiciously.

"So forget it, then." Walsh shrugged.

Willow glared, snatched up the wad of paper, smoothed it out, and looked for the bottom line. Her heart skipped a beat. She grinned at Walsh and found him grinning back at her. "A horse race?" she said. "Sixty dollars cash for the winner! Whew! How come you didn't tell me right off? Why, I'd do almost anything . . ." She chewed her lip, grew thoughtful. "Brother, do you think Eagle and I have a chance of winning that prize money, really?"

"She's got mustang blood in her, remember," Walsh reminded smugly.

Willow nodded. "True. But I've seen some awful good-looking horses in this country, thoroughbreds, some of them. Eagle probably ain't got a chance. But . . ." Willow straightened herself up taller. "You're right. Eagle's ma and pop were wild mustangs up in the Smoky Hill country. Those horsecatchers never would have captured Eagle when she was just a three-day old foal if her ma hadn't been fighting off a mean old range bull," Willow mused. "They never did catch her ma—"

"That was real good luck, that rancher, Mr. North, giving you your own horse for keeps, that time," Walsh said with envious disbelief, even after all this time.

Willow looked at him, feeling a warm glow as

she remembered. Her voice came soft, "Eagle was so little and wobbly and white as snow." She repeated the old story, though both of them knew it well. "Mr. North thought my dog, Blue was his name, was killing his sheep. We were Mr. North's neighbors. He shot Blue, killed him. He found proof later it was a coyote doing it. He felt so bad about shooting my dog, he gave me the little white foal Eagle to keep for my own. Papa told Mr. North he didn't have to give me the little foal, it being a mistake, but he wouldn't have it no other way. And he paid some cowboys a good price for her, too."

Walsh sighed. "Jingles ain't got energy enough to even make a body suspicious he was chasing something—get killed." He sounded half-wishful.

"Walsh!" Willow almost screamed, "don't be stupid. I'm glad I got Eagle, but I loved my dog Blue, too, don't forget it. You love Jingles, too."

Walsh looked ashamed. "Awright. Awright. Are you enterin' the race?" he asked, rotating his shoulders before going back to his hoeing.

"I might. I'll see what Papa says, at supper."

"*Yah*," Papa agreed that night as they ate by lamplight. "We go to celebration Fourth of July, if wheat is all in shock by then. Got a ragtag threshing crew coming here, around the tenth. We go, but don't count on winning horse race, daughter. Hard work, that get us Ranch, not racing horses."

Mama smiled, her face across the table from Willow looked almost young and pretty in the shadows. "*Oui,* our family go for the good time. How they say? 'All work, no play, make Jack stupid.' "

"Something like that, Mama," Willow said with a laugh, "and you're right. I hate to admit it, but I wouldn't mind getting clean away from work, have some fun, for just one day." She nodded. "I'll enter Eagle in the race, win or lose. You never can tell. I'll see she gets exercised a lot till then. Shocking wheat is going to wear me out, daytimes. I'll practice running her when it is cooler, after night chores. Even if I am wore out, I can sit in the saddle and hang on."

A few mornings later, Papa drove the big, mule-drawn binder into the wheat field, Willow and Walsh trotting close after. The big machines, sickles *whirring,* windlass turning, made a wide swath along the edge of the field of yellow gold. Willow loved watching the blades catch the grain stalks, lay them into the cutter. One by one the stalks fell onto the canvas conveyor and were carried up, to disappear into the mouth of the binder. With a clank and clatter of gears, the first bundle of ripe grain came spitting out—rolling into the swath just cut.

Willow and Walsh fell to, lifting the bundles and standing them upright, twelve bundles to a shock. It was slow hot work, but behind them rows of golden shocks grew. Under this hot sun, Willow believed, filled with hope, it would be no time before the shocks would be mature and be ready for the threshers. If they could work faster. . . .

Toward the end of the second day, Willow talked Jessamyn into helping, to speed things along. But Jessamyn wasn't in the field long when she lifted a bundle of wheat to hear the warning, angry *br-r-r* of a rattlesnake. Walsh got a pitchfork and killed the snake fast, before anyone could be hurt. But Jessamyn, white-faced, ran for the house with skirts in hand and no amount of insistence from Willow could bring her back to the field.

Giving up, Willow admitted to herself that Jessy couldn't help it, maybe, being a person who just didn't fit in the fields. For a fact, Jessy did a whole lot better with her sewing, baking, writing poems, dancing her own made up dances—things like that. She and Jessy weren't much alike, but that was all right. Who wanted to be peas in a pod?

Even doing without Jessamyn's help, by the time the moon came up on the night of July third, the wheat was all in shock. "Look how beautiful it is," Willow whispered to Eagle as they skirted the field in a canter, their practice runs over for the night. "All those shocks, so neat and tidy, like they were just marching along in the moonlight. Reminds me of the words to a hymn:

'Onward Christian soldiers, marching as to war.' "

She gave the pony a pat. "It's true, too, that wheat is going to help win the war in Europe, and it's going to help us Fabers' war to have a place all our own." Willow stifled a weary but contented yawn. "Well, little horse, it's time to give you a good rubdown and some oats. Tomorrow's your big day, the Fourth of July. Going to show folks around here what a fast little pony I got, aren't you?"

Morning came too soon; Willow felt only half-ready for the day. Would she do all right in the race, win? She did chores with Walsh and Adan's help. Then Papa brought the mules, Jen and Ben, in from the pasture and hitched them to the wagon for their trip to the Seena Picnic Grove.

When the others had gone ahead into the house, after chores, Willow sat down for a moment on the stone curb of the ancient well to think, calm herself before the big challenge ahead. A dewy-sweet smell rose from their newly stubbled fields. Feeling almost like a little kid, Willow had a silly urge to wink back at the sun. Laughing, she ran to the house, her bare feet fairly dancing on the dusty path.

Mama was at the stove, fork in hand, turning pieces of chicken that sizzled loud in the big iron skillet. Jessamyn was stuffing boiled eggs at the side table, and Laurel, alongside Jessy, drowsy-eyed and yawning, was buttering an enormous stack of sliced fresh bread. Amanda sat in a chair not far from Laurel.

"Smells good everywhere I go this morning!" Willow exclaimed, getting a bowl of mush for her breakfast from the pan of it on the back of the stove.

"Even that *eau de cologne* you brought in on

you from the barn?" Jessy asked in mock sweetness. Jessamyn's hair was freshly washed and it curled softly around her face, the waves in back were gathered and tied with a white ribbon. If Willow didn't miss her guess, Jessy had also pinched her cheeks to make them rosier.

Willow grinned and looked down at herself. She had to admit there was near a week's worth of barn and field filth on her clothes. Jessy should try staying clean doing the kind of work she did! But even if her overalls were spanking clean, Mama wouldn't allow her to be seen in public in them. Which was going to make riding in the race not so easy.

Fiddle-deedee, Willow told herself silently as she ate, *I'm going to be in that race if I have to ride like that Lady Godiva did on her white horse. Naked except for her long hair!*

There really wasn't two sides to the decision. Willow put on her good yellow dress with black polka dots, after a quick bath, and was ready when the others piled into the wagon. She saw that Papa had tied Eagle's reins to the back of the wagon. Willow gave the white pony a swift hug, a soft word of encouragement for what lay ahead of them, then climbed up into the wagon to sit beside Jessy, who looked like a flower in her pale pink frock.

The big mules pulled them along at a good clip. Almost to the grove, Auberta Steele's black Maxwell automobile roared around the Faber wagon, enveloping them in an enormous dust cloud. "Git a horse!" Walsh bellowed.

In a flash Mama's knuckle came around to clip Walsh's head, "Mind manners!" she scolded, reducing Walsh's loud laugh to a snicker. Although she said nothing, Willow told Walsh with her eyes that she sided with him.

Someone must have decided that the grove of cottonwood and elm trees wouldn't make enough shade for the large numbers attending the picnic. Willow noted that two big bowers had been built in the open field near the pond. Long forked poles had been driven into the ground, with lighter poles laid across. On top of everything were leafy branches, no doubt cut from trees along Johncreek.

As Papa headed the team and wagon toward the far end of the grove, Willow saw a stage under one bower, with important-looking folk beginning to find their places in a row of chairs. They'd make speeches after the flag raising and band music, according to the handbill Walsh had given her.

Under the other bower was a long table for eating picnic dinners out of the sun. Which was getting hotter by the hour, Willow thought to herself, pushing a damp lock behind her ear.

Willow looked back at the swarms of youngsters splashing in the pond, and she heard a familiar voice squeal, "But it's so dirrteee." It was Melinda Lewis, pretty in a bright red bathing suit. Farley Baxter, looking like a fat biscuit in a tan swimsuit, held Melinda's hand. A half-dozen other boys Willow recognized from school, including handsome Reid Evans, looked eager to take Farley's place leading the squealing Melinda into the greenish, shallow water.

A strong wish to be with them, right there amongst the laughing gang in the water, made Willow's heart beat faster. She half-rose from her seat on the bench in the wagon, then settled back, hoping the family hadn't noticed.

Suddenly, she saw Conroy Gill appear from nowhere and slip up behind Melinda. Willow caught her breath, seeing Conroy scoop Melinda into his arms and throw her out into the middle of the brackish pond. There was a big splash, then Melinda came up sputtering, her hair dripping mud, her red suit now a burnt-orange color.

Willow tried not to laugh, feeling sorry for poor Melinda. Being pretty and popular could have its side of trouble, too.

Finally, Papa pulled the team to a halt. The Fabers leaped from the wagon and scattered. Willow found a patch of grass under a lone giant mulberry tree far back in the grove, and she tethered Eagle there. "We're going to win today, aren't we girl?" Willow said, caressing the white satiny neck. "What do you say?" Eagle nudged Willow's shoulder and nickered softly. Willow giggled. "That's what I thought!"

Willow wandered through the grove without aim, impatient for race time to come, but enjoying the respite from work. The horse race was set for late afternoon, final and most exciting event of the day, if you didn't count the Grand Ball to be held that night at Johncreek School. The Fabers wouldn't attend the dance. It had been decided that none of them really had clothes suitable to wear to a ball. Willow smiled to herself, remembering Jessy's wail, "Oh, for a fairy godmother!"

Even if Jessamyn were old enough, who would ask a tenant farmer's daughter to a ball? It didn't matter, though. Things were going to change, be different for her and Jessamyn, someday soon.

For a long while, Willow stood and listened to the speeches about liberty and justice and such. Seymour Lewis, Melinda Kay's father, was fourth on the list of merchants, politicians, and well-to-do farmers making Independence Day lectures. Willow listened to Mr. Lewis's glorious oratory thoughtfully. His words seemed empty to her, and a lie, somehow. She decided it had something to do with the black man fanning the sweating banker, running glasses of water to him, that threw the speech out of kilter.

At noon, Willow joined Mama, Papa, and the younger children seated on quilts spread in the dappled shade of a cottonwood tree. Willow soon dropped the drumstick she'd hardly nibbled back onto her place. "I'm sorry, Mama, this is the best picnic dinner in the history of the world, but I'm just not hungry. I think I'll go check on Eagle, give her some water."

Mama clucked her tongue and motioned for Willow to try harder. Papa, though, reversed the command with a lenient shake of his head and waved Willow off.

On her way to the mulberry tree, Willow saw Eliot and Egbert Abraham and called "hello" to them. Passing within two feet of them, she said "hello" again, but they couldn't hear her, due to their loud disagreement about whose turn it was to lick the ice cream freezer paddle that Eliot held.

Shaking her head, Willow laughed softly and went on. She saw to Eagle's water, then sat down at the foot of the mulberry tree, her legs tucked under her skirt as she chewed thoughtfully on a stalk of yellowed grass. Did they have a chance today, an honest-to-goodness chance to win, she and Eagle? She reached up to pat the long nose that rested on her shoulder. She wished she wasn't so nervous.

"Nice pony," a boy's voice drawled suddenly above her.

Willow's head jerked up. She got to her feet fast. "Uh, I didn't hear you come up—you scared me some." The boy before her was wearing faded overalls, he was shirtless—his broad shoulders and bare feet were nutshell brown. Willow looked up into vivid blue eyes and felt her heart suddenly beating faster. A shank of the boy's dark curly hair lay across his deeply tanned forehead; his grin was easy-going, kind. "Are—are you from around S-Seena?" Willow asked. "I—I don't think I seen you before."

He shook his head and snapped his fingers at a blue tick hound nosing about a bush some distance away. "I'm from Long Lane, Missoura. Name's Frank Tucker," he told her.

"Oh!" Willow said with a wide smile, "I know your great-uncles, the Abrahams. They own The Ranch, the place we farm. We intend to buy it from them soon as we can."

"Then your name is Faber," Frank Tucker said.

"Willow Faber." She remained silent a moment, feeling strangely short of breath and quivery. "I hope —you—like Kansas," she said finally, "and living with your uncles. They're nice. We get along with them just fine."

"They're a little different," Frank said with a twisted grin, "but Uncle Eliot and Uncle Egbert are good old guys. Living with them's going to be okay. They don't care about living fancy. I don't, either. I like to hunt, fish, and explore around." He took a few steps forward to run a hand along Eagle's shimmery white hide. "Nice horse," he said again. "Wish I could've brought my chestnut horse Fiddler with me. Guess I was lucky I got to bring Ol' Blue there." He nodded at the hound that had come to lay on the ground nearby, tongue out, panting.

"Your dog is named Blue!" Willow exclaimed with a surprised smile. Standing beside Frank, wishing she'd taken the trouble to meet him long before this, Willow told how she came to have Eagle, because of her dog named Blue.

"This pony's a good runner, I bet," Frank stated in the form of a question, turning to Willow.

"She's so fast when she runs she almost flies, that's why I call her Eagle. I'm going to enter her in the big race today," Willow said. "I'm hoping to win the sixty dollar prize money, put it with our savings to buy The Ranch—we're having a dickens of a time getting enough to—" Willow broke off, suddenly aware that Frank was giving her an odd stare. "Wh-what's wrong?"

He looked away from her, then back. "You can't enter the race," he said with an apologetic sigh.

Willow frowned, puzzled. "Sure I can. They—they wouldn't hold it against me—our—our being tenant farm folk—not in a horse race."

"No." Frank shook his head. "It ain't that. It's cause you're a girl. I heard the judges, and others, talking. The big race will be for men and boys only. I heard them say that if enough girls want to, they'll hold a separate race for them, after. But with no prize money in that race."

"They—they can't do that," Willow sputtered in disbelief. "Are you sure? That's not fair!" Her head spun dizzily. "They can't do that. I have to be in the race. I could have stayed home, worked today, but I came to win the race, or try to. Do you know what I mean? They can't keep me out of it because

I'm a girl!" Willow turned away from Frank Tucker, trying to smother down her feelings that were close to the boiling point. How could they? It just wasn't fair!

seven

FRANK said nothing, but Willow was well aware of his presence close behind her. At last he spoke, "How about me riding your pony in the race? I'd give you the prize money if I won."

Willow thought it over, shook her head. She turned slowly. "Thanks. But Eagle is a one-person horse. She'll run her best only for me. It would have to be me that rides her." Willow looked at the ground and bit her bottom lip to stop the quivering.

"I'm sorry," she heard Frank Tucker say quietly. "The way I see it, a horse is a horse and a rider is a rider. I don't think it's fair, either, that you can't ride in the race just 'cause you're a girl. But I didn't help with the rules."

Willow didn't answer. She turned and buried her face in Eagle's mane for a moment, then she looked over her shoulder at Frank. "I—I have to think about this. Do—do you mind? I'd like to be by myself awhile."

"Sure." He snapped his fingers, and Ol' Blue was instantly on his feet, tail wagging, face grinning.

"We'll see you around sometime? I sure am sorry," he said again.

" 'Bye," Willow whispered. "See you." Her eyes followed Frank Tucker's lanky, straight-backed form, the blue tick hound trotting at his heels, but her mind was on the race. She had to be in it. She *would* be in it, but how?

Willow walked and walked, trying to think of something. She passed the sleeping form of Seymour Lewis, stretched out under a tree, snoring, his folded coat under his bald head for a pillow. The speeches must be over then, she thought. Mr. Lewis and Owen Gill, Conroy's Pa, were among the judges for the race, along with the honorary judges, the Abraham twins and Auberta Steele. Could she maybe get them to change the rules? The twins might, she decided, but they'd be outnumbered by the others, who wouldn't.

Now, time moved too fast. Willow strode about, trying to think. The hour for the race grew closer and closer. Suddenly, like the clear ringing of a bell, it came to Willow what she must do. She moved quickly into a run, her eyes searched frantically the knots of people she passed, looking for Walsh. Her brother! She had to find him!

It seemed forever passed before she located his chunky figure in a crowd about an ice cream freezer. She should have known. Walsh stepped forward to take his turn at cranking the handle just as Willow snatched at his collar. "Walsh," she yelled, "come with me, quick."

"No." He shook her fingers loose. "I'm helping. I get some ice cream for helping."

"Come with me!" Willow ordered, pulling him away, "now. Come on, it's a life or death emergency." She dragged at him frantically, her desperation giving her added strength he could do little about.

"Willow," he cried, trying to fight off her hands, "it's banana. Real banana ice cream."

"I know—you'll get some, maybe later," Willow told him, hearing the pleading in Walsh's voice. "Right now you got to come with me."

Unable to do otherwise, Walsh gave in and Willow rushed him through the crowds to the mulberry tree where Eagle waited. Good, Willow thought, nobody back here. Lucky she'd kept Eagle away from the noise of the main crowds. "Now." She faced Walsh. "Take off your clothes."

Walsh stared at her and took a few steps backward. "You're loco."

"No, I'm not, Walsh. But some dumb judges are." Quickly Willow explained the rules of the main horse race. "I have to ride in it," she said. "That's what I came here for. But I got to look like a boy." She grabbed his straw hat, then began to unbutton the front of her dress, changed her mind. Maybe she could keep the dress on. "Get your pants off, give them to me."

"Willow," Walsh said in a hoarse whisper, "don't take my clothes. This is stupid. What will I wear? Don't Willow, please," he begged, "what'll I wear?"

"Your birthday suit! Give me your overalls! Now listen," Willow said in a kinder tone, "I'll turn my back. Take your overalls off and hand them to me. Shinny up in that tree where the branches are leafiest and stay up there until the race is over. That's all you got to do. *I* got the hard part."

"Willow," Walsh was close to sobbing as he handed her his overalls, "you hadn't ought to make me do this."

"Give me your shirt." Willow paid small attention to Walsh's distress. She whipped the shirt on over her dress and attempted to stuff the shirt, dress, and her petticoat, inside the overalls. It was too much, she wouldn't hardly be able to walk, so stuffed. Time was running out! Willow took the shirt back off, removed her dress, then put the shirt on over just her petticoat, tucked in the tails and hooked the suspenders of the overalls. Better. She pulled on Walsh's straw hat and tucked her long dark hair up inside.

"There." Willow picked up her dress and rolled it into a ball. "Keep this up there with you. Do I look like a boy?" She could make out Walsh's flushed face nodding as he peered, owl-like, down at her from several feet up in the leafy tree. She tossed him the dress and went to saddle Eagle.

In another few minutes, Willow mounted and was ready to go. As she rode away, she heard Walsh hiss after her, "Soon as that horse race is over, you get right back! Hear me, *Willow whip?*" She stiffened in the saddle. So that rotten nickname was getting around? Her brothers and sisters probably called her Willow whip all the time behind her back. One of these days . . . !

Everywhere Willow looked, she saw signs that the race was about to start. From the road, and from areas of the grove, riders were pointing their mounts toward the far side of the pond, where a crowd was gathering. Willow urged Eagle into a lope and joined the other riders, reminding herself to keep her straw hat pulled low and not to speak to another soul lest she reveal her girl's voice.

As she rode, she looked about her slyly for some other member of her family but saw none of them. Just as well. They would recognize Eagle and her, and wonder what she was up to dressed like this, maybe spill her secret accidentally.

There was a delay as one rider changed his mind and went back for a different mount.

Then, finally, a big, bearded man with a voice like a foghorn bellowed orders, "All right, gents, get your horses up here to the starting point. Line up straight. Move over, some 'a you so everybody's nose to nose an' every horse's got an even break. Yeah. That's right. Now, when I fire this here pistol," he waved the gun, "it's ever' man for himself. Ride yonder straight west across this open field to John-creek. See them little black buggy looking things over there, yonder 'cross the field? That's the judges, fellas, waitin' for y'all at the finish line, just this side the flour mill."

Willow's throat grew dryer with every second. Her heart pounded so hard she wondered that everybody couldn't hear it. From the corner of her eye, she tried to study the other horses, worriedly guessing which of them might be the fastest. She was sure by the look of some of the mounts that Eagle could beat them. Others she wasn't sure about. Like the Chickasaw pony—the dancing, head-tossing Indian pinto. Never could tell about a horse like that. The Chickasaw had plenty of wild blood in him, like Eagle, you could see it. The cowboy riding the pinto looked as if he knew what he was doing, too. Another horse that might be hard to outrun, Willow decided, examining from under the brim of her straw hat, was a black stallion on her far right. Above its glistening hide and prancing white feet was a prosperous-looking rancher who sat easy in the saddle.

In the next second, at the edge of the waiting crowd, Willow saw Mama and Papa. Of course they'd be watching the race. From the lift of Papa's head, his folded arms and one hand fingering his moustache Willow could tell he'd figured things out and now just wanted to see what would happen. Mama was wearing her "just-wait-til-I-get-my-hands-on-that-girl" look. Feeling sick inside, Willow was beginning to wish she'd never heard of the race—when the pistol cracked.

Of their own accord Willow's legs automatically squeezed Eagle's sides. The pony lunged forward in a gigantic leap. "Yi-yah! Ha-ha-ha!" Willow shouted as she stretched low over the white neck. She let the reins go slack to give Eagle her head. "Fly, little girl, fly," she crooned in a whisper, "take us home, take us home to win."

Under her, Willow could feel Eagle's powerful muscles in smooth, ground-eating motion. The wind whipped at the brim of Willow's straw hat but it didn't come off. From the corner of her eye, Willow saw the black stallion's nose come even with Eagle's. She snapped a look over her shoulder and saw the Chickasaw pony pounding up close behind them. The other horses didn't even look to be in the race. "Go—go—go!" Willow chanted softly. "Go my Eagle, fly!"

Ahead of them, the "black bugs" were growing in size, taking the shape of people. Willow's eyes burned, her ears filled with the thunder of hooves on hard ground as the black horse edged forward; other horses sounded so close she felt they might go over the top of her. The stallion's black neck stretched out. They were ahead of her and Eagle.

Willow's heels poked Eagle's flanks, and she begged, "Fly, little white Eagle, fly! We can do it—we can do it." Under her, Willow could feel Eagle moving out faster and faster. They were in front now—if only she and Eagle could hold the lead—!

There was tumultuous yelling, all around her screams of encouragement, gleeful laughter, then someone shouted, "White horse wins!"

Willow's heart shouted what her lips couldn't say aloud with people close by, "I love you, Eagle, I love you so much."

She didn't see where the dog came from, it was suddenly *there* directly in front of Eagle. The pony skidded to a halt so quick Willow sailed over her head in the same instant. Before she hit ground, Willow realized what could happen . . . her hat. Her hands went up to hold it on her head and without her hands to break her fall, Willow hit the ground with all the force of being dropped off a shed roof. Sharp pain zipped through her right shoulder. She rolled, staggered to her feet, and fell to the ground again.

"Hey, son, wait a minute! Let us help you," she heard a man shout.

"I—I'm all—all right-right," Willow grunted in a deep voice. She tried to get to her feet alone and shook off the hands that reached to help her. She limped about in an effort to show those watching that she was, in truth, just fine. She shook her head to clear the dizziness. Why didn't they just hand her the prize money and let her go? The pain that blazed in her shoulder set Willow's teeth on edge. She hoped no one noticed that she held her hurt arm stiff against her side.

"Something wrong with your arm?" a kind voice asked. "Better let me take your shirt off and have a look at it."

"No!" she choked. "I'm fine." Willow shook her head. She made her voice as gruff as possible, and without looking up said, "I—we won didn't we?"

"You won, fair and square." At those words Willow felt a pang of guilt. "You were acrost the finish line when that dog came up and caused your pony to spill you. Let's get back to the picnic so you'll be awarded your sixty dollars in front of all those folk over there. What's your name, son?"

"Wil— Will Faber," Willow growled.

She kept looking at the ground and stumbled to Eagle. It seemed forever passed before she was again in the saddle. She could make out three men on horseback flanking her, it sounded as though the honorary judges were getting into a buggy for the ride back to the picnic. Willow sneaked a look ahead, across the open field, as they rode. She drew a quick breath when she saw the yelling, clapping crowd weaving in the shade at the edge of the grove. She uttered a silent prayer for help to get through the time ahead.

As they neared the grove, Willow spotted a strange apparition separate itself from the waiting crowd. It came toward her. Willow blinked, shook her aching head, and hoped what she saw wasn't true. It was. The yellow and black polka-dot dress came steadily on, faster and faster, stomping bare feet below, short-haired red face above, now yelling,

"Willow you stupid girl, how come you didn't come back? I waited and waited."

"You dunderhead," Willow muttered. "Walsh, you're a dunderhead."

People were beginning to laugh at Walsh wearing her dress, a sound that grew and bloomed until it sounded like a town-sized chickenyard of cackling hens.

"You're a girl?" the rider nearest Willow growled in disbelief. "A girl? Now what're we going to do?"

After a hesitation, Willow sighed, reached up, and pulled Walsh's hat off her head, allowing her hair to cascade to her shoulders. The soft wind eased the dull ache in her head and cooled the perspiration on her brow. "You should have waited," Willow said tiredly to Walsh, who now walked alongside her and Eagle, muttering dark threats under his breath. "We were slow starting, somebody had to get a different horse. If you had any sense at all, you'd have been patient till I got back."

The man who rode closest to Willow still complained, "I don't know what to do. I sure don't know what to do now. This changes things—you being a girl. You understand that, don't you? This sure changes everything."

"I know it does," Willow replied with a sinking heart, hearing the unavoidable exasperation in the man's voice. She had been so close to holding sixty dollars cash in her hand. There was no hope for it now, thanks to Walsh. Willow looked at the rider escorting her.

It was Mr. Owen Gill, Conroy's father, who owned the livery stable and wagon works. As she studied the stocky man in western garb, dark-skinned like his son, he turned to the other riders and sang out, "This here winner's a girl. What we gonna do about that?"

They reached the shade of the grove. Willow slid from the saddle and leaned against Eagle. She ignored the shouted comments and heated wrangling that filled the air. Maybe they wanted to hang her, she didn't know. Willow waited for strength to return to her wobbly limbs and for her mind to clear. After a while, a hand touched her shoulder ever so lightly. Willow looked up and saw dark-haired Frank Tucker, a faint grin on his tan face.

"Nice ride, *fella*," he said, teasing. "You feeling better, yet, from that spill? Better perk up. I think the judges are almost ready to make an announcement you ought to hear."

Willow stared at Frank a moment, then she hung onto Eagle's reins and stumbled after Frank as he motioned her toward a knot of people a few yards distant. Some of them grinned in her direction, still others shook the hand of the rancher who rode the black stallion. What was going on? Willow stopped where she was, closed her eyes, and shook her head.

"Come on over here, little girl," Mr. Gill called,

"and get your prize. You get half, missy, thirty dollars. The judges agree they ain't seen a better ride in many a moon than yours. But rules is rules, you are a gal. So half the prize money goes to the rider who come in second, Mr. Jordan, here."

"You got a fine pony, young lady." Mr. Jordan, the rancher, congratulated Willow with beaming admiration. "You'd have won the whole pot if the rules were what they ought to've been. If they'd let me, I'd give you this thirty dollars, too. Your horse earned it."

"You're right about Eagle," Willow said, "she did earn it. But I broke the rules. Thirty is—" She shook her head. "Thirty dollars is near a fortune. Thank y-you."

Eliot Abraham tottered up and clasped Willow's hands warmly in his own withered palms. "We wanted you to have it all," he said.

Egbert squeezed in close to Eliot and gave Willow a resounding kiss on the cheek. "What a ride, youngster!" he cackled. "Beautiful pony, too. Both of you should go to California and be in those new moving pictures!"

Willow laughed with delight, then sobered as Seymour Lewis jostled the elderly twins out of his way, "Now, young lady," he said, "we're awarding you half this prize, but we don't go along with cheating. I wanted a second race; I tried to get my Melinda to get a group of you girls to hold a second race for you to ride in, but none of them wanted to. That's part of the reason we are giving you half the prize. The other part is—you're a rider, young lady, a real rider, and that should count."

It seemed to cost the banker a lot to say it, so Willow did her best to look modest, and ashamed of her wrongdoing. A wedge of townsfolk and farmers, her classmates out in front, moved up to offer Willow their congratulations, and to admire Eagle as she unsaddled and rubbed the pony down. Willow looked for Mama and Papa, half-worried, then saw them off to the side, waiting with her brothers and sisters. Papa looked proud enough to burst; Mama didn't look nearly so upset as earlier. Willow grinned to herself, glad for their pleasure in her.

Walsh wasn't with them. He was probably at the mulberry tree, Willow reflected, madder than a whole nest of hornets as he waited for his overalls. What was the hurry? Her numbness was fading. It would hardly do for her to turn her back on all these folks being so kind, would it? Walsh deserved an apology, and her thanks, and he'd get them. Soon.

Auberta Steele shoved forward, grabbed Willow's hand in a calloused palm, and commenced to wring Willow's sore arm from its socket. Willow winced and tried to withdraw her hand. "Thought you won whole hog, didn't you?" Auberta blatted like a sheep. "I voted to disqualify you. Don't hold with cute shenanigans, myself. But—it was a middlin' ride. Middlin'."

"Th-thanks," Willow said through clenched

teeth. She hoped the spinster wouldn't render her arm useless, what with threshing waiting for them at home. She would like to tell Miss Steele what she planned to do with her winnings, for spite, but she didn't. Partly because she was afraid of what the spinster might do if she knew the Fabers' plans to buy The Ranch.

THE stiffness and pain in Willow's arm went away just in time. At daylight on the tenth of July, the threshing machines came clanking up the road. The great, black, whistling steam engine with separator hooked on behind was herded through the Fabers' gate by a shrewd-eyed, black-bearded man in tattered striped overalls and denim coat. The rest of the harvesters, three rough but able-looking young men in their early twenties, came after in three mule-drawn, rumbling box wagons.

Nearly breathless with excitement, Willow stayed by Papa's side like a burr as he dashed hither and yon to show the crew where he wanted the strawstack to be and thus, the separator. The black engine was unhooked and set some distance away.

As the work commenced, it drew Adan, even, from his treasure dig in the grove to watch their wheat harvest. In short order the crew was driving overflowing wagonloads of shocked wheat up close to the waiting mouth of the great chugging machine. Whips cracked, dust flew, men shouted. The threshing machine's canvas conveyor was like an enormous tongue licking up the bundles of wheat into its gaping mouth.

Willow laughed at the loud rumbling and gnashing of teeth from the machine's innards, then waited with held breath to see the first blast of chaff and straw fly from the blower pipe. The younger children whooped and hollered at her heels as Willow raced around to the other side to watch the first golden grains of wheat flow from the chute into the waiting empty wagon.

Later, feeling so proud she almost ached, Willow took her place on the wagon seat to drive their first load of threshed grain to the Seena warehouses where it would be weighed, paid for, and stored for an eastern buyer. It seemed to her different this year —it was more *their* wheat, from *their* land, because of their intentions to buy The Ranch.

On her second trip to Seena with a load of wheat, Melinda Lewis hailed Willow from the sidewalk. "Hello. Would you like to come to a party at my house this afternoon? Everybody's coming. It's going to be a watermelon feed; we're going to play croquet on our lawn, dance, you know. Frank Tucker is invited, he suggested we ask you."

Willow drew her team up. "Yes. No. I mean, yes I'd like to come. But, no, I can't. We're right smack in the middle of wheat harvest. I have to help." She waved and clucked her team on.

"Suit yourself." Did Melinda calling after her sound glad she refused, Willow wondered. Or did she imagine it? The young people from school had been real nice to her the Fourth of July after she won the horse race.

A shadow of worry dimmed Willow's high spirits. She hadn't thought about it at the time she decided to work harder than anything to help buy The Ranch, but working all the time was going to keep her from making good friends. She'd be spending her time, night and day, on The Ranch. Maybe, working like that, she'd get to be such a dullard, nobody would want anything to do with her, anyway. Willow lifted her chin. She'd figure out something, straighten out this problem, though it'd be a hard nut to crack.

By noon that day, Willow was too tired and hungry to give consideration to anything but her stomach. In the kitchen, Mama and Jessamyn worked furiously to get the meal on the table, looking weary themselves in their clean, sweat-damp print dresses. But her mother and sister had a proud look, too, as they spread the table with large bowls of boiled chicken, bowls of egg dumplings, platters of fried beefsteak, and ample amounts of every kind of garden vegetable they grew. The harvest crew was silent, eating as though there would be no tomorrow. The craggy men's exaggerated eye-rolling and lip smacking when they tasted Jessy's raisin pie sent the young ones into fits of giggles.

Under a burning cobalt sky, the harvest continued the rest of the afternoon. To Willow, tired though she was, it seemed harvest was over almost before it had hardly begun. By lamplight in the kitchen, the same night, the harvest crew was paid and the great machines clanked and rumbled off into the dark.

Because of her respect for Papa, head of the house, Willow didn't ask exactly how much of their money went into the yellow crock—after the crew was paid—but it looked to her like a fair amount. Feeling glad, she dropped on her bed and slept like a rock.

eight

Late in the month of July, Jessamyn baked a feather-light white cake and Mama served it with sliced peaches and thick fresh cream, in celebration of Willow's fourteenth birthday.

This is so good, Willow decided, sitting with the family at the kitchen table, eating her birthday cake. That silly worry she had had a while back, about being a drudge, not knowing how to have fun—there was no reason for feeling that way. This past month, her birthday month, had been practically perfect. The horse race, for instance. And meeting Frank Tucker, the Abrahams' nephew. Of course she hadn't seen him much since, but she might, again. She'd had to work right along when they harvested the wheat, miss that party, but the harvest itself couldn't have been better. There was that to be glad about.

"I think everything's going to be all right." Until the others at the table laughed, looking at her strangely, Willow wasn't aware she had spoken aloud. She covered up quickly, "What I meant to say is, 'This cake is just the best, Jessy.' "

It was a stifling hot night a month later, in late August, when Willow sat on the porch watching the fireflies that looked like dim little lamps in the dusky evening. The only sounds to break the stillness were the fluttering miller moths bumping themselves against the lamplit kitchen window screen, and farther off, the heart-rending, *"coo, coo,"* of mourning doves. Hot as it was, she still liked doing nothing at all tonight.

A movement at Willow's feet made her look down. "Jingles! Hardly ever see you anymore, with you always under the house out of the sun." Jingles licked her hand and whined. She stroked the brown cur with affectionate sympathy, thinking that these "dog days" the heat was hard on all their animals. The chickens, the livelong day, stood with wings out from their bodies, panting. They were losing their feathers from sunburn, and Mama worried that they would stop laying eggs altogether. The cows had slacked up giving milk, too.

The weather had to cool down soon, or they would have a peck of troubles. They couldn't get along without Mama and Jessy's butter and egg money for everyday needs. Under Willow's comforting hand, Jingles's head came up and he growled low in his throat.

"What is it, boy?" Willow whispered. She squinted to see what was coming toward them in the gathering dusk.

An angular figure loomed in the yard and swept toward Willow. "Who—? Miss Steele?" Willow gulped, surprised. She got to her feet. What could the spinster lady want with them? Willow drew herself taller and swallowed once more against the growing dryness in her throat.

"Pesky skeeters!" the woman barked as she came into the lamplight spilling from the window. "You don't keep moving, they'll eat you alive. I want to talk to your pa, girl, where is he?" Mosquitos landed on Auberta's chin like dark hairs. With a swish of her hand she wiped them off. "I ask where your pa is?"

"In—in the kitchen with Mama," Willow answered, curiosity and worry making her voice faint. She motioned with her hand. Auberta Steele shoved past her, lifted a fist to pound on the screen door, then, not waiting, she yanked the door open and marched inside.

"How are you folks doin' this evenin'?" The spinster's voice carried back out to the porch to Willow. "Ain't this heat awful, though? August in Kansas brings out the worst of everything."

Willow sagged back to sit on the step. She nodded in silent agreement. "It sure does," she whispered, "including you." Willow didn't want to go inside where there wasn't a spare breath of air. But she must know the reason for Auberta Steele's visit. Willow moved closer to the screen door, rested her back against the weathered boards of the house, and strained to hear.

She thought the spinster would never get to the point. The woman's droning voice made fuss about the heat, mosquitos, and the corn crop at such length, Willow was ready to yell at the spinster to get on with it.

Finally, Miss Steele barked, " 'Going to Emporia for a few days while things are slow on my place. Want to buy some stock, and I expect to look at some machinery I been needing. Maybe I'll see a picture show and ride the streetcars like the dimwitted city folk do. Thing is, Faber, I could use you to see to my stock, my farm, while I'm gone. Ain't a lot to do other than the milking. I've been watching what you are doing here on this place, and I figure I can trust you to do things right. How about it? I'll pay you a wage—'course it won't bust the bank." Auberta Steele roared with laughter at her own weak joke.

Papa, work for Auberta Steele? Stuff and nonsense! Outside, Willow held her breath, wondering, waiting for Papa's answer. There was pay offered, though; that was something to think about.

Papa asked a few questions. "*Yah*," he said after a while. "I do it. I help you. Not much work on our place now, either. My Willow Sabrina can take care of most of it. *Yah*, sure, I help."

Willow slapped at a mosquito stinging her arm

and grinned to herself. Maybe it was a good thing.
Mama was anxious to begin sewing school clothes.
Miss Steele's money for Papa's choring could go for
dress goods, and maybe shoes, too, if there was
enough. They wouldn't need to rob the yellow
crock. Willow got to her feet quickly, shoved her
hands in her overall pockets, and humming happily,
headed for the moonlit pasture for a few minutes
with Eagle.

Who would have thought a lucky break would
come to them from Auberta Steele, of all people?
Willow chuckled and buried her face in her pony's
ghostlike mane.

Papa was away at Auberta Steele's each morning
and night chore time the following week. Willow,
feeling proud of Papa-the-wage-earner, didn't mind
her added responsibility at home. Besides, Papa would
be home all the time come September, when they
needed him most. That's when they'd start shucking
corn and working up the fields for planting winter
wheat.

Starting the first of October, she would be off
to school, daytimes, at the academy. It was still like
a dream, that she would be going on to high school.
Mama and Papa, though, wanted it as much as she
did, they said. Willow decided she would go all out
for a change, to try and make friends, be one of
the regular bunch. She'd pretty herself up more, for
one thing. It'd be nice to get out of these overalls

and into pretty dresses more often. Maybe she should fix her hair a different way, too?

ONE NIGHT, Papa was later than usual coming home for supper from Auberta Steele's. Willow paced back and forth, following a worn ridge on the old kitchen linoleum. How could *she* be so patient? Willow looked at Mama seated in a kitchen chair with the faded pair of overalls she was patching draped across her knees. Working, always working at something, Mama. Jessamyn's pretty face was bent over a muslin blouse she was embroidering with tiny pink flowers; sewing for herself, but that was all right.

Under the table, Laurel, Adan, and Clay played jacks. The little red rubber ball and tiny metal stars were tossed out, then gathered up, then tossed again as they chattered. Above them, Walsh nodded sleepily over a tattered old book about Abraham Lincoln's boyhood.

"Shh," Willow told baby Mitty with a smile. Mitty, tied as usual into her high chair with a towel about her chubby middle, ignored Willow with a grin, and gurgling, continued to bang her tray with a wooden spoon. To Willow, the banging spoon seemed to toll the passing time, an unwanted reminder that Papa was now well over an hour late.

"Ain't Pa home, yet?" Walsh came blinkingly awake and lay his book down. "I'm getting hungry."

Willow chewed her lip. "Don't know what could be keeping him. Only that Auberta Steele's

got a sow about due to have a fall litter. Could be
the sow's farrowing early and she is having trouble
of some kind. Papa would stay until everything is
all right."

Under the table, Adan, who sometimes showed a
ghoulish appreciation for unpleasant matters, blew the
hair out of his eyes and stated with a wicked grin,
"Old sows lots of times eat their own young'uns."

Willow saw Jessamyn give Adan a withering
look of disgust. Little Laurel's eyes filled with sudden tears as she looked out from under the table.
"Do sows really do that, Mama. What Adan said?
Do they really eat their own cute piggies?"

Mama seemed only half aware of Laurel's question, but she looked up from her patching. Willow
realized that Mama, too, must be starting to worry
about Papa. "Shhh, *chérie*, don't cry," Mama murmured to Laurel rather absentmindedly. The little
girl's face was a knot of distress until Mama went
on, "Papa, he is there. He not let bad thing like that
happen."

"See there!" Laurel said, relief in her voice as
she socked Adan's shoulder.

"Stop!" He shoved her hand away. "Mama,
can't we eat? My stomach keeps roaring like a lion."

"We eat," Mama said with a wan smile. "Come."
She put her patching in the basket by her feet and
motioned to the girls to help her put supper on the
table.

There was sizzling fried potatoes, steaming corn

on the cob, and a large platter of ruby-colored sliced tomatoes, bread and butter, and milk. It was one of Willow's favorite meals, but the food could have been wood and sand, she was so worried about Papa. Papa'd been late other times. But tonight she had a deep inside feeling that something was bad wrong. She hoped it was only her imagination.

After supper, Jessamyn automatically washed dishes and Laurel dried them with few words, although they usually argued first about whose turn it was to do which. Willow helped, to have something to do.

"Maybe I should ride over to Miss Steele's, see what's keeping Papa?" Willow suggested as she hung up the damp dish towel to dry.

"*Non.*" Mama shook her head. "Papa, he is come soon. Is the pig keeping him, I think." Mama's smile was meant to reassure, but it hadn't skipped Willow's notice that Mama's sewing had been lying limp and neglected in her aproned lap for some minutes now.

The littlest ones were put to bed. Willow, Mama, Jessamyn, and Walsh waited in the kitchen, each pretending to be occupied. A soft thud and moan sounded from the porch. As though yanked by a common string, the four of them were on their feet, racing for the door.

"That you, Papa?" Willow cried. She shoved the screen door open. In the ghostly moonlight,

Willow made out the huddled heap on the porch, Dulcie waiting riderless by the step.

"*Mon Dieu!*" came Mama's soft cry of alarm, beside Willow. In seconds Mama was kneeling on the porch by Papa's crumpled form. "Karl," she said, "my love, my life—" She choked. "You are bad hurt?" Mama's hand went to Papa's head, and her fingers came away with a dark stain. She looked at Willow, her pale face set with fear. "My children," she said, "you must help me get your poor papa to his bed. He is black out."

Slowly, carefully, the four of them managed to get Papa inside. There was a soft chorus of indrawn breath when the lamplight showed too clearly Papa's bloody head and his blood-soaked shirt. "I'll put on a tea kettle of water," Jessy whispered as they got Papa onto his and Mama's bed. She rushed back to the kitchen. No sound of crying came from Mama, yet tears glistened on her cheeks as she knelt by the bed and examined the cut on Papa's head in the light from the lamp Willow held close. Walsh left, and Willow knew without her brother's saying so that he had gone to see after Dulcie, Papa's riding horse.

"We sew up Papa's head ourselves," Mama said, without looking up. "You must help, Willow. You—you can?"

Still numb from previous shock, now Willow's heart seemed to stop. Her throat was dry, hurting. She'd never known Mama to sew up a wound on a person before. Animals, yes—chickens, dogs. All of them got better, and lived, but. . . . "Mama," Willow said aloud, "I will go after a—a doctor. I'll saddle Eagle and—"

"*Non*." Mama stood up. "Real doctors live too far away. We must do for Papa. I care for Karl, myself."

Willow hesitated a few seconds longer, then nodded, shivering. She couldn't be like this if she was going to help Mama. She pulled her hands into tight fists, swallowed hard, then let out a long sigh, and let her hands go loose. "All—all right, Mama. W-what do you want me to do?"

Mama covered Papa's quiet form with a blanket and patted it around his shoulders. "We need the Lysol for to clean wound. A pan of hot water. I sterilize needle over fire in stove. In a hot oven we put thread and towels to sterilize."

A horrible thought struck Willow and her shaking began all over again. She whispered, "Mama, is Papa—? Are you sure Papa—?"

"Oh, *chérie*." Mama's voice caught. "Papa lives. But you must hurry!"

Not once did Papa stir while they worked over him, but he breathed with a slow, steady rising and falling of his chest. Willow felt worried to the very marrow of her bones. Would Papa be all right? What had happened to him? What had hurt him so?

It was done. Filled with limitless admiration, Willow had watched Mama sew poor Papa's wound with the steadiest hands she had ever seen. Willow could only guess how much Mama had had to make that calm efficiency happen. It was she, Willow, who finally put the lamp on a table and reached for a chair, positive that her legs wouldn't hold her a moment longer. Now that Papa's head was bound in the sterilized cloths, there was nothing to do but wait.

"Karl," Mama murmured every few minutes, "you hear me? Karl, wake up."

Seeing there was nothing more for them to do, Walsh and Jessamyn followed Mama's orders and went to bed. Adan, Clay, and the baby had been quiet in their beds, asleep, for some time. Willow's own eyes, though they hurt, would not close. She brought her chair to sit close to Mama, by Papa's bed. Her worry for the silent form on the bed increased by the minute. Was it her fault, wanting The Ranch so badly, that caused Papa to get hurt? Would Papa have chored for Auberta, otherwise? She knew he would have, just to help out. That's how Papa was.

"He such a good man." Mama's soft voice broke into Willow's thoughts, as though they'd been thinking exactly the same thing. "He want your Ranch as much as you do, you know." Mama went on, her voice sounding as if it were coming from far, far away. "When we courting, in old country, in his land where we meet, he tell me we own our own land, someday. 'For you I get it all,' he promise.

He mean it, too. Then . . ." Mama's voice trembled and faded away.

Willow waited, feeling very close to Mama, loving her, wanting her to go on and tell her everything about when she and Papa were young. "What happened then, Mama?"

"We come to America, for new life, to have family."

Something—the proud lift in Mama's voice, made it simple for Willow to picture the two of them getting off the boat. Papa, a lean, not very tall, blond farmboy, holding the hand of his dark and lovely seventeen-year-old bride. In his other hand he carried the old satchel, holding everything they owned. Being so young, they were scared a bit. But both of them anxious and excited about what they wanted to do, about the life they would build in the new country they had chosen.

Mama's soft chuckle of embarrassment broke into Willow's thoughts. "We have three dollar and ten penny when we come to America. Can you believe? Make good new life on three dollar and ten penny? Your Papa go to work, on dock at first, then on farm. Work ver' hard. He dream to own the land, so bad he want."

Mama sighed. "You come *chérie*. Then other babies, bing, bing, bing. The money to buy land never there, it take all to care for our chil'ren. We love our babies. Papa, he stop look so far ahead in future, stop dream of owning land. He look ahead harvest to harvest, yes, day to day, working other man's land. It not hurt that way."

Listening, Willow began to understand how much Mama and Papa had wanted the same thing she did, long before. It was the reason they had come to America in the first place. It must have been born in her, then, from them, this need she felt for the family to have a place of their own. "We'll get The Ranch for Papa, for me, for all of us, I swear, Mama," Willow said in a rush.

Mama chuckled softly again. "Always the young they not afraid to dream big, dream far. Is good. Karl, Karl, my sweetheart, wake, please."

Much later, Mama's hand reached for Willow's. Willow's sagging eyelids flew open wide, for Mama was smiling in quiet, joyful relief. Mama stood up and leaned over Papa's bed and Willow was right after when she saw Papa's moustache move, his eyelids flutter.

"Ach," Papa groaned, "my head. Oooo. Julie? Willow, daughter? Why do you look at me so funny? I—I need drink of water."

Willow couldn't help it, she laughed. "Oh, you, oh, Papa!"

It seemed Mama couldn't stop nodding. "So. He be all right. *Bien! Bien!* Bring your Papa a nice cup of cool water, Willow."

When Papa stayed awake for several minutes

and looked better, Mama questioned him, "Karl, what happen? The cut on your head, how you get it?"

"Ay, remember," he dragged out. "*Yah*, sure. Ay was in Miss Steele's barn, chust finishing chores. Something hit me on the head. Ay think *barn roof*, maybe. *Ay* black out. When I wake up I see this kaffir corn knife had fallen down on me from where it was hanging on rafter—not hung up good you can bet! I cuss Miss Steele's good-for-nothing hired man, before me, for that . . . !" Papa's voice faded, his eyelids fluttered and closed. He reached shaking fingers up toward his bandaged head.

"Rest, Karl," Mama said. "You no talk more tonight."

But a few minutes later, Papa whispered, "I had bad time getting home. I black out two, three times. Finally catch Dulcie, get saddle on her. Everything get fuzzy, black, coming home. I don't know nothing for a while. Then I wake up again. I keep coming, but sometimes I don't think I get here."

"I'm sorry, Papa, I should have gone looking for you, Willow said. "We were so sure Auberta Steele's sow was in trouble having her litter and that was what was keeping you. I wish I'd gone looking for you, Papa."

A wobbly smile touched his lips. "Tomorrow I be up good as new. *Yah*. Is all right, daughter."

Papa couldn't have been more wrong, Willow decided a few weeks later, than if he had announced he was going to take Mr. Lewis's place as head of Seena's only bank. No matter how hard he tried, Papa couldn't put in a full day's work plowing and harrowing, without several worrisome dizzy spells. The spells left him weak as a kitten, and Willow worried not only about Papa, but wondered in near panic what might happen to their plans to buy The Ranch.

She'd promised Mama, she'd promised herself, she'd sworn to everybody that they'd have The Ranch. And she finished sowing their winter wheat alone, with Jen and Ben pulling the wheat drill she rode, or seeder, back and forth across the black earth. Although she wanted to believe otherwise, deep down Willow knew her work was not on a par with Papa's. She could hardly wait for spring—for a showing of green in the field to tell her how well she had done.

October first and the opening of the school year was coming up fast. To Willow, it seemed the more she felt she ought to stay home, help all she could on The Ranch, the more she ached to go to school. Torn, unable to decide, Willow took her problem to Mama and Papa.

The younger children, Jessy on down, had gone to bed. Mama and Papa and Willow were in the kitchen. Mama was clearing the worktable, Papa sat in a chair close to the stove, smoking his pipe thoughtfully. Willow, trying to help Mama, was mostly getting in the way. "You go to school," Mama said firmly without even stopping to look at Willow.

"You go! Always later, if it not work, you can stay home."

"Is good for you to go to school," Papa agreed. "We manage."

Tears Willow didn't expect went splashing down her cheeks. She wiped them away fast. "Oh, Mama, Papa, you don't know how glad I am. I— I guess I didn't really know, myself, how much I wanted to go on to school, to that new Seena Academy where all the kids will be. But I do. And I won't quit on you, on us, getting The Ranch. I can do a lot, here, before and after school, and weekends. Everything will work out—I'm sure it will."

It was a golden Indian summer day outside, the first day of school. Willow sat at a table in the school's wide entry hall, trying to complete a registration form for enrollment in Seena Academy. Her face, bent studiously over the card, was scrubbed shiny; she'd pinned her hair in a wad of curls on the back of her head, and she wore a violet print dress that carried a smell of new cloth.

Name. Address. It was hard to keep her mind on the blanks to be filled out. Did she look enough like the others, Willow wondered. Were her clothes, her hair, right for here, high school? She felt strange, different from her summer self, somebody new, somebody else. Scared.

Oh, she should have stayed home. They needed her there. Why did this noisy mob, her glance zigzagged around the room, matter so much to her? Farley, Melinda, Reid, Conroy, and that good-looking Frank Tucker sitting over there? She made herself stare at the registration card. She had to finish.

Ambition? the final line asked. Willow's brow knit as she tried to bring order into her jumbled mind. What did she want to be, do? Design beautiful houses, did girls do things like that? Or, how about being a farmer, a good one? She'd like that, but only if she could do it without getting coarse and ugly like Auberta Steele. Wife and mother? Willow chewed the end of her pencil. Probably, but how could she know for sure about that now?

What I want most to be is a real regular person here where I am. No, no, she couldn't write that as her ambition. Because it was the only line she left blank, Willow didn't feel guilty. It would have to do. She lay the pencil down carefully beside the card and smiled at no one in particular. She was in school. Her second year in Seena.

Hip hip hurrah!

nine

*A*s the days passed and the deeper chill of late autumn set in, all the Fabers found themselves working hard, although Willow took the heaviest work load for herself.

Each morning the family dressed in darkness. It was Walsh's job to light the fire, lamps, and lanterns, fill the woodbox, and with half-hearted help from work-shy Adan, feed and water the chickens, clean the coops, and feed the pigs their corn and slops. Mama's right-hand, Jessy, got Mitty and Clay up and washed and dressed them, then with Laurel's help she set the table for breakfast and made the beds while Mama cooked breakfast and set bread dough to rise.

Willow milked the cows, fed the larger animals, cleaned the barn, then headed to the cornfield for an hour or two of shucking corn before school. The ears drummed into the box wagon as fast as she could toss them, and would, as long as she could keep it up, she'd decided.

Willow knew, while they were at school, Mama worked herself near to a frazzle redding up the house, cooking, sewing, washing and ironing clothes, and keeping watch on the two littlest ones. Holding out as long as he could, Papa tended to what chores he could complete during the day. He banked the foundation of the old house with straw against the coming winter chill, shelled corn in the barn, and close to the warmth of Mama's kitchen stove, he oiled and repaired worn harness and tools.

Each day, after school, the chores of the morning were repeated, with the addition of cleaning and filling lamps and lanterns for Jessamyn and Laurel and a few hours of shucking corn for Willow and Walsh. It was often nine o'clock at night before Willow and the others could spread their books on the kitchen table for an hour of homework by lamplight.

It seemed to Willow it had been forever since she had enjoyed a good night's sleep. She tried, but her work on The Ranch piled up. She got further and further behind in her assignments at school. It would change as soon as Papa got his strength back, she kept telling herself. It had to.

One night in mid-October, after chores, Willow headed for the house, dreading the mountain of homework waiting for her there. Suddenly, she heard footsteps coming up the lane, someone whistling. Willow's heart skipped a beat, and her cheeks warmed. She'd heard that merry whistling before, in the schoolyard, and a couple of times in Seena.

She set her lantern on the ground and waited. The light from Frank Tucker's lantern bobbed toward her.

As he approached out of the dark, Willow could see that Frank carried a gun on a sling over his shoulder. Dressed warmly, in one hand he carried a lantern and in the other he gripped a small axe. Old Blue whimpered excitedly at his heels, drawing Jingles from the barn. The dogs sniffed one another curiously, then began to zip and dart about in play.

"Goin' to battle Indians?" Willow asked Frank, with a nod at his gear.

"Naw," he laughed, " 'coon. Uncle Eliot and Egbert've been telling me about some oak-tree-filled gullies southwest a way. Going to check 'em out for 'coon. Thought—well—thought you might like to go hunting with me. Walsh, too, if you want—"

For no reason she could think of, Willow's face turned hot and she was glad it was too dark for Frank to see. She drew a deep breath and closed her eyes for a second. How long had it been since she'd done a thing purely for fun? Too long ago to remember. Last Fourth of July? She would like to go with Frank, oh, how she would. But there was all that homework to be finished. Time for morning chores would be here before she got even a few winks of sleep—it seemed that way. Willow's feeling of yearning, to go with Frank, have a good time, switched without warning to resentment—boiling, unreasoning, anger.

"Haven't you got anything better to do?" Her voice was like rocks hurtled up at the boy's face, staring wide-eyed at her. "Night hunting is for owls, not folks with good sense." Willow knew she wasn't being fair to Frank, but now her tongue was loosened she couldn't stop. "Why aren't you home looking after your uncles? Or in bed where you belong, or doing that rotten assignment in language Mrs. Isling gave us today? What do you want to go traipsing around with a fool dog, for? And a gun you'll probably blow your head off wi—" Frank bent his head and pressed his cool mouth for an instant on hers, ending her tirade. Utterly stunned, Willow took a backward step.

"I—I had to make you—you shut up," Frank stammered, "but I didn't know—I was going to do that, to do it." He hesitated a moment longer, as if to say more, then he turned and hurried away.

Still in shock, Willow watched Frank go. Then, a flood of frustration, pain, and apology welled inside of her. "I'm sorry!" she whispered into the empty night, "I'm sorry for everything that is." She ran toward the house. Her lantern threatened to blink out as she whipped it along. But when she got to the house it was still lit, burning as bright as the warm glow beginning to grow inside her. Frank. That crazy boy had kissed her!

Willow took her language book to bed and tackled the assignment, her last one, determined to put everything else, especially Frank, out of her mind. The lesson said to choose one poem from several offered and write two full pages telling what the poem meant to her. Willow chose a poem about early pioneers finding a new life, a poem that spoke of their struggles, their goals, their never giving up. She could understand that. It was a lot like Mama and Papa. Willow read the poem through three times. The pages almost wrote themselves.

When she woke next morning, Willow saw with relief that she had remembered, somehow, to blow out her lamp, but she had gone to sleep with her cheek against the cold pages of the language book. She crept from bed, feeling so stiff and tired it was as though she hadn't slept at all. The one good feeling she had was about Frank. Might as well admit it—maybe the kiss was meant to shut her up, but she had liked it all the same.

Shivering, Willow yanked on her clothes and rushed to the kitchen to get warm. The stove was cold, she discovered, groaning. Mama, in her bulky tattered robe and gown, lighted a lamp. "Where's Walsh?" Willow asked irritably, "how come he isn't up?"

"He was sick in the night," Mama said, turning the lamp wick higher. "Not bad sick, but Walsh not go to school today."

"And I'm stuck with all the chores!" Willow grated. "It'd be a fool's pipe dream to count on help from Adan." So cold her teeth chattered, Willow got into Papa's heavy coat, picked up the clean milk pails, and went outside.

Mama's soft, *"C'est la vie,"* followed Willow out. *That's life.*

Was Mama sorry for her, or was it a warning?

After breakfast, Willow found that Eagle had thrown a shoe and she would have to walk the four miles to the academy. With a lump in her throat that could have been caused by her hastily gulped breakfast, or weariness, or a mixture of both, Willow set out on the long walk. She was coatless, her books were tucked under her arm. Her outgrown coat now belonged to Jessy, but blamed if she'd wear Papa's ugly old barn coat to school just to keep warm. Not when a boy, *the boy*, had given a sign he liked her, cared enough to kiss her, even when she was talking awful to him.

Willow's fast walk and the warmth of her wool jumper were not enough against the cold. Long before she reached school, her teeth were chattering and her nose and cheeks were numb. The cold mud of the road was turning her toes to ice inside her worn shoes.

It could have been worse, though. She was glad for the wine-colored jumper that Mama had made recently from an old dress washed and turned wrong side out so the material looked new. In a roundabout way, the jumper was payment from Auberta Steele. The spinster had thrown in a pile of clothing as a bonus to Papa because he got hurt in her barn while she was in Emporia. Jessamyn wanted nothing to do with the "rags," as she called them, but her eyes showed surprise and envy when Willow paired the new wine jumper with last year's cream-colored blouse for a pretty new outfit. Willow had been surprised herself, looking in the mirror. It wasn't often she felt pretty these days—it was like looking at a stranger.

As she neared school, thoughts of Frank crept into Willow's mind. She shouldn't have yelled at him last night the way she did. It wasn't him she was mad at in the first place, it was . . . just everything. It was always having to work, never having a minute to spare, have fun. In order to get The Ranch, she couldn't be hardly any different than Jen and Ben— work brutes. It was her choice, though. It was The Ranch she wanted.

Willow turned at the sound of rattling harness and creaking wheels behind her and saw an approaching horse-drawn buggy. It was Doretta Lawrence, finished with her mail route, late for school, too.

"Like a ride?" Doretta called when she came alongside, and Willow quickly nodded. Doretta drew up and Willow climbed to the buggy seat beside the big blonde girl. "Honey, you look colder than a corpse," Doretta said in husky-voiced sympathy.

"I—I'll l-live," Willow answered through chattering teeth. She put her books on the seat and hugged her body with both arms. She had often wondered how Doretta, only a year or two older than she, had come to carry the mail, of all things, and now she asked.

"It was my daddy's work, for years, till he died. Every Tom, Dick, and Harry from these parts had the mail route after daddy died, but one after another they went away to war. So it's my job now. I live alone with my mother on our old place over Johncreek way. Don't do much farming. Mother hasn't been the same since Daddy died of pneumonia, but we get by on butter and egg money and my pay for delivering mail. How about you? You haven't lived very long on the old stagecoach place, have you?"

"No," Willow said with a shiver, "but we expect to live there from now on. We're fixing to buy The Ranch." The two of them chatted companionably the rest of the way to school. Willow began to feel better. This day that had started out so bad: Walsh sick—choring alone—no coat to wear except Papa's extra one, which she couldn't make herself do, mightn't necessarily turn out the same way.

A welcoming rush of warmth met Willow as she entered the tall brick school, and she vowed never to let herself be this cold again. Maybe Mama would let her wear her Sunday coat to school. Willow spotted Frank Tucker's lanky, blue-overalled figure a short distance ahead in the hallway. Her heart skipped a beat. She moved faster, hoping to have the nerve to talk to him about last night.

She'd behaved like an awful dummy, though;

what could she say now? Willow hesitated, slowed. Maybe Frank wouldn't like for her to bring up last night? He hadn't meant to kiss her, it had surprised him as much as her. She'd leave it up to him, then. If he truly liked her, he would let her know in his own way, wouldn't he? Except for telling him she was sorry for yelling at him, which she surely intended to do, she would wait for him to start whatever came next.

In class after class, Willow worked extra hard at her assignments in order to get as much done at school as possible; there was so little time for homework at The Ranch. At the end of language class, Mrs. Isling returned Willow's essay she'd written the night before, about the pioneer poem. Willow covered her mouth, resisting an urge to shout out loud, when she saw the large red $A+$ scrawled at the top of the first page. That proved it—she could keep up with school and work at home, too!

But, in the weeks that followed, Papa mended so slow, and Willow oftentimes had to bully the younger ones into helping her when she couldn't get all the work done alone. "Willow-the-whip" they taunted her time after time, but more and more Willow was able to close her ears and mind against the hated nickname they'd tagged on her.

Now and then Doretta Lawrence came to visit Willow. Fortunately, the older girl took pleasure in tackling a large share of whatever work the Faber family was doing, mostly corn shucking now. Her visits didn't slow a thing. Rather, her funny jokes and stories made the hard work of picking corn seem more like play, and Willow welcomed Doretta, anytime.

One Saturday afternoon in November, hearing the creak of wheels coming up the drive, Willow, in the barn, thought it might be Doretta. She snugged a blanket close around the tiny premature calf she'd been tending and hurried eagerly from the barn.

It wasn't Doretta. Willow halted, stalk-still, and stared at the oddly mixed group seated in kitchen chairs in the box wagon—her eyes of their own accord found Frank Tucker first. Then she saw Auberta Steele holding the team's reins, and the elderly twins, Eliot and Egbert Abraham, muffled to their eyes, in back. Willow guessed that Auberta's fancy auto was froze up at home, too troublesome to start, the same with the Abrahams' car. But what had brought these folks here, together? Willow clutched Papa's coat tighter about her and took hesistant steps toward the wagon.

She answered Auberta's and the Abrahams' greetings and led the way to the house, her mind a jumble of frantic wondering. She felt Frank looking at her, but Willow's sharpened worry wouldn't let her forget the others and speak directly to him.

Mama rushed their guests into the front room, the tidiest room in the house, and brought them coffee, apologizing with actual pain that she had no fresh-baked pastries to serve with it. Papa joined them, settling carefully into his chair, whatever he was thinking hidden behind the gentlemanly manner with which he regarded their guests. Willow stood by the stove, tense, as she waited for someone to get to the point of this strange visit.

Auberta Steele needed no prodding. "Faber," she barked, without the courtesy of a "Mr." as usual, "you got hurt in my barn and I feel accountable in a small way. I own an old house in Seena, on Mulberry Street, near the tracks. It's been empty a long time. I want you and your family to have it, rent free, till spring!"

A house in town? Free? They *lived* here. . . . Willow couldn't grasp Auberta Steele's meaning, but something about the spinster's gloating, purposeful manner frightened her.

Papa's eyes went into a squint, his moustache twitched. "What you talk about, ma'am?" he asked.

The spinster gave him a plastered-on smile of fake cordiality. "It's like this, Faber. You see, I want to *buy this place.* I met a good man in Emporia who'll farm it for me, along with the rest of my place. He will want to live here." Auberta Steele continued, purring almost, "You'll be better off, mending in town, Faber. When you're fit, of course, come spring, you'll want to go looking for another farm to rent. I hear in Cherokee County—"

"No!" Willow gasped. Auberta Steele wanted them off The Ranch, wanted them to move into a town shanty? Willow knew the house, it was a crumbling heap that would blow down in the next strong wind. What gall the woman had!

Mama, who'd come to stand close beside Willow, gave the barest whisper, "I'm ver' tired of move, move all the time. I wan' to stay."

Willow waited for Papa's reaction, feeling as though a heavy weight was settling down on her; she actually sagged, and her hand came too close to the radiant sides of the stove and she was burned. She yanked her hand back and pressed it hard to her trembling lips. Papa, she thought silently, Papa, please say something! I can't, you're the head of the house.

Eliot Abraham leaned forward in his chair. He turned his hat nervously in his gnarled fingers. "Miss Steele come to us, but we didn't want to give her an answer until we talked to you, Mr. Faber. We want to know your feelings about this."

Willow had liked the old gentleman before, now she liked him even better. She turned toward Egbert when he started to speak.

"We won't kick you out or anything like that," Egbert added with a shake of his grizzled head. "No, no, nothing like that. Brother and I ain't so old and addled we don't know you are doing wonders on this place. If you want to stay, we know you aren't well, Karl, but . . ."

Papa, it's your turn, Willow thought, feeling a flicker of relief, *tell them.*

At that moment, Frank Tucker stepped out of the dim corner where he had been standing and halted between his old uncles' chairs. A young man. "We know how much you folks want to buy The Ranch, or did," he said earnestly to Papa. "If you still want to, that's fine. Uncle Eliot and Uncle Egbert talked to me about it, and that's what the three of us decided—you'll still have first chance if you want it."

Auberta Steele protested quickly, "You got rent past due, but you won't have to pay it for the months you've lived here. I'm tackin' that amount onto the offer I'm making the Abrahams." She threw out her scrawny chest and took a long draught from her coffee, smiling like a pleased cat over the rim of the cup. "All you got to do is move." It was one of Mama's nicest cups, with violets painted on the sides, and Willow wanted to snatch it from Auberta's hand.

Papa still hadn't spoken. Willow looked worriedly at him, and was startled to find him looking at her, somehow measuring her. After the longest time, Papa reached up to touch his head, feel the old wound where the hair was growing back. "I get better every day," he said calmly, "and I got my girl, Willow. She is hard worker." A proud, quiet smile filled his face. "*Yah*, sure, she works as good as most farmhands who get pay. I don't change my mind. I pay rest of rent that is due when Willow sells corn. We have down payment a few months more. There's no worry. We still want The Ranch." Papa stroked his corncob pipe, the expression in his blue eyes unruffled, his smile calm. That he considered the matter settled, was obvious.

Following the tension of the past half-hour, Willow's knees felt like melting butter as intense joy coursed through her. She wanted to say something, to hug Papa, but she felt she might fall if she moved. She felt Mama's work-roughened hand reach over to gently squeeze her fingers.

"If that's what it's going to be," Auberta grunted, "*if—*" She stomped across the room, a pinched look on her face as though she smelled skunk cabbage. At the kitchen door she turned to the Abrahams, who rustled along after her, both looking pleased with the turn of events, but kindly trying not to show it too much. "Boys," Willow heard Auberta hiss, "if Faber can't swing the deal he's talkin' about, my offer stands."

The elderly twins shared a look of dismissal, but said nothing aloud.

Frank Tucker nodded farewell to Willow, and she sensed something behind his grin, something probably like what she was feeling this minute. Her cheeks warmed. "C-come over some time," she invited. He nodded. His grin was on the shy side, but the light in his eyes told her he was more than a little bit pleased.

With help from Doretta Lawrence and Frank Tucker, the corn picking was finally finished. One cold, bright Sunday afternoon, Willow made time to go horseback riding with Frank. His uncles' gray mare, Belle, had trouble keeping up with Eagle, and in fact might have gone to sleep if Frank hadn't kept prodding her. Willow had her hands full trying to hold her white pony back from a spirited run. She felt guilty that she didn't take Eagle out for exercise more often. It couldn't be helped, though. There was so much work to be done on The Ranch, if they were to have it for keeps.

Willow and Frank rode along until they came to the railroad tracks that split the town of Seena, then turned and followed the tracks in a southerly direction until the town behind them, when Willow looked back, looked like a jumble of children's play blocks. There was a toy cloud of smoke over the town, from numerous burning leaf piles.

Not wanting the peaceful afternoon to end, Willow agreed to ride on until finally they reached a meandering, deep-banked river with thick stands of trees along either side. "Now that's treasure," Willow mused, staring at the trees; "more so than in Adan's grove."

Frank caught up, released Belle's reins, and blew into his cupped red hands. "Did I hear you say something?" he asked.

"I was just thinking about all those black walnut trees, there," Willow told him, her heart beating faster. "I'd bet a dollar to a doughnut that nuts from two or three trees would fill a wagon. They look half-dried already, those on the ground. They'd need to be hulled. Cracked, and the nutmeats picked out, they'd sell—to somebody."

Frank laughed. "Crack black walnuts? Might as well try to crack stones. You can spend an hour getting half a handful of nutmeats."

"Which makes them worth more," Willow retorted, her voice rising. "Listen, Frank, the holidays are coming. I have an idea that Farley Baxter's dad would buy black walnut meats from me to put in all those baked goods he'll be fixing for his Thanksgiving and Christmastime customers. He might pay for them real good. Won't hurt to ask, anyhow, and I'm going to."

Frank sat his horse and watched her, silent. There was a quizzical smile on his mouth and something like admiration in his eyes that Willow saw and was glad for. "Every penny counts at our house these days," she admitted. It would be embarrassing, too personal, to tell the Fabers' money troubles to just anyone, but she didn't mind telling Frank. "Mama counted our yellow crock savings last night. We're doing fair, but we have to do a lot better."

"So you're going to have a nut business? It fits," Frank teased.

For a second, Willow missed his meaning, then she blushed, and eyes flashing, said, "Go ahead and laugh at me, but I bet I have the last laugh. Us Fabers will do anything, as long as it is honest, to get The Ranch."

Frank's arms flew up to cross protectively in

front of his face. "Wait," he yelped, "wait! I'm on your side. I'm not Old Lady Steele, out to get your ranch."

Willow had to laugh. "Lucky for you, you're not," she told him. She liked Frank more and more all the time. He hadn't kissed her again, since that one time. He probably wouldn't, either, not for a long time, anyway. It seemed right to her, to not rush such things. She smiled at him. "Let's go home, funny friend."

The following Monday, after school, Willow rode Eagle into town to talk to Mr. Baxter, the baker.

ten

ILLOW left Eagle ground reined, hurried up the steps of the bakery, and opened the door. A bell tinkled as the door opened and closed after her. Willow shut her eyes and sniffed. Heaven, she decided, her mouth watering, probably smelled like warm vanilla, chocolate, and yeasty baking bread.

At a sound, her eyes flew open. Mr. Baxter, a large man dressed all in white, stood behind the main counter. His pleasant face, round and shiny-red like his son's, was floury. Willow smiled at him and explained her mission, quickly, because his manner, while not unkind, seemed hurried. "I'll supply all the nutmeats you need," she finished, "cracked, picked, and ready to use."

Mr. Baxter took no time at all to make up his mind. "We will give it a go," he told Willow with an agreeing nod. "Old Mr. Shaugnessy and his wife Mag used to keep me in shelled black walnuts." He shook his head. "They both passed on to their reward last spring, died within a week of one another! I'll give you twenty cents a quart for meats." He raised a hand. "But I want them fresh, no shells."

"Fresh, no shells," Willow promised. "Thanks a lot, Mr. Baxter," she said, shouting almost, for he was already bustling into his backroom heaven.

Willow rode home to The Ranch, whistling "Redwing." She was so grateful for this new way to earn money, she was scarcely aware of the cold and the round of chores that waited for her in the barn.

The very next Saturday, Willow drove a wagon back to the black walnut trees. Mama and the younger children came, too, heavily bundled against the cold. Jessamyn stayed home to cook dinner and care for the baby, Mitty, while Papa stayed behind to shell seed corn in the barn.

Under Willow's directions, Walsh shinnied willingly up each tree in turn and shook the branches. Except for Willow's and Mama's watchfulness and constant nagging, four-year-old Clay would have followed Walsh to the top of every tree, or tried to.

"I'm coming down, Willow," Walsh called finally, "that's all that will shake loose." He joined the others under the trees, scuffling through the leaves, stooped as they picked up the nuts and dropped them into their sacks. They'd been working for some time when Willow noticed Clay sitting silent at the base of a tree some feet distant. His small face, dirty and tear-stained, was filled with hurt and disappointment. His fingers picked at a patch on the knee of his grubby overalls.

Willow's heart went out to him. "Come on,

Clay," she called, "this is a family business. We can't do without you." Several minutes later, Willow discovered Clay, a small, quiet shadow, picking up nuts directly behind her.

Other families began to arrive with their wagons, but Willow saw that there was more than enough to go around. Her only troubling worry was that Mr. Baxter might forget his promise to buy from *her*.

In the days following, each night before bed all the Fabers gathered at the kitchen table to crack black walnuts. From scraps of iron in the barn, Papa made two viselike tools that made the nutcracking easier. But, because picking the meats from the shells was tedious and difficult, it still took an hour or more to fill one quart jar with nutmeats.

When the first ten quarts were ready, Willow took them to town.

"Fine, keep them coming!" Mr. Baxter told her as he counted out the cash payment for the walnut meats. "I can sell some as they are, here on the counter, to folks who want to do their own baking at home. And a friend of mine in Emporia, with a bigger business than mine, will buy them from me if you can keep them coming."

It was much better than she'd hoped! "No worry about that," Willow said. "You bet we can keep them coming." Her promise to herself not to let anyone see her stiff, sore, discolored hands forgotten, she held them out to accept the money. She put the bills and coins away carefully in Papa's worn leather coinpurse, which she'd brought along for the purpose, and assured the baker again, "We'll bring you more black walnuts, lots more."

On one of her trips to Seena to deliver nutmeats, November eleventh, Willow was surprised to see knots of people talking excitedly on every corner. The saloon was doing a roaring business. "War's over!" she heard gleeful shouting. "The Germans surrendered. The big war's over!" The holiday feeling was like a contagion spreading through the town. Smiling to herself in surprise, Willow saw that businessmen didn't care whether they had customers or not. Townspeople that she knew to be usually prim and proper were dancing in the mud of the street. Willow managed to make her transaction with the baker, who mumbled about "folks still need bread to live." She too, would be glad to get away from the craziness and back to the quiet of The Ranch.

Come Thanksgiving morning, Mama fretted aloud, wishing she still had Chandler to stuff and bake for their holiday dinner. But adapting as always, she gave a last sigh of regret and turned full attention to killing and roasting a tough old rooster instead. Willow's feeling of guilt was short-lived.

Cold December brought no lessening of activity at The Ranch. Besides the usual barn chores, housework, and school, there was corn shelling in the barn, nut cracking in the kitchen, and chopping wood in the shed against the coming winter storms.

In an icy corner of the girls' bedroom, Jessamyn

curtained off a workroom. With skilled practicality, she spent her spare time there, creating Christmas presents for the family from odds and ends. Willow didn't argue when Jessy insisted that no matter how important it was for them to buy The Ranch, it was every bit as important for the little ones not to be disappointed on Christmas morning. It was hopelessly crowded in the bedroom, but Willow was only too glad to go along with Jessy's plans. They wouldn't have to turn to the yellow crock savings. Because of the nut venture, the amount was looking better and better.

Papa and Willow set aside enough corn for spring seed, choosing the most deep-grained. Not long after, Willow sold the rest of the corn at the Seena warehouse to pay off the balance of the year's rent to the Abrahams. And Auberta Steele paid another evening call.

Willow thought it might be her imagination, but it seemed to her that the spinster was disappointed because Papa looked so well. With a deep frown on her leathery face, Auberta jerked a chair up and sat down at the table where the family had gathered for their habitual two hours of cracking nuts. "Heard you had a fair corn crop, Faber," she barked. "Well, that's this year. Nobody knows from one day to the next how things'll go on a farm. It's nip and tuck. A big gamble, that's what farming is. Takes a stout heart to stay with it. Get a good crop, then suffer a loss on the next, that's how it goes." For an hour

Auberta clacked on, voicing doom, not giving anyone else a chance except to nod or exclaim.

From time to time, Willow darted a worried look
at Papa, to see how he was taking it. She was glad
at last, to discover a twinkle in his blue eyes, although his mouth, behind his moustache, looked serious enough. With the tine of a fork, Papa pain-
stakingly picked a meat from a rough, crinkled, black
shell.

It came to Willow that something was going
on, a secret, not out in the open. A soft choking
sound came from Walsh, and Willow looked at him.
The boy's face was beet red with held-in laughter,
his chubby body jerked with chuckles he was trying
not to let go. Willow stole a quick look at the gabbling spinster—for that was where Walsh seemed to
be looking—and she saw what was ticking Walsh's
funny bone to a frenzy.

The spinster, no doubt so used to keeping busy
she didn't realize what she was doing, had taken a
paring knife in hand and was picking nutmeats
from cracked shells. She dropped them swiftly into
the jar centering the table. Her nimble fingers
flashed, causing the nutmeats in the jar to grow at
an astonishing rate; all the while her lips moved at
the same speed, mouthing words that were plainly
intended to discourage them from buying The
Ranch!

Willow swallowed, choking back her own
laughter when she saw that the entire family was

atune to what was taking place; without knowing it, the spinster was helping the Fabers buy The Ranch.

Auberta Steele came to her point after what seemed forever, "I have a different plan from the one I had when I was here last time," she said brusquely. She tossed a nutmeat into the jar. "Faber, you look to be coming along pretty good, after that crack on the head. I'll buy this place and take on all the worries that go with ownership. You can run it for me, Faber, if you and your family are so set on living here." From the look on Auberta's face, she was with some regret offering them a gold moon tied with silver ribbons.

Papa's smile was gentle, his voice quieter than usual as he answered Auberta. "Ay give my word to my daughter, Willow, don't you understand? And to my wife and little children, we try hard to be landowners, ourselves. This place, for them. *Yah,* sure, you don't want me to break my word to such a nice family I got, do you? Our chance may never come again." He shook his head. "*Nay,* I'm sorry."

Papa's gentlemanly firmness, the look of unified agreement on every Faber face, large and small, around the table, was like a fuse to Auberta Steele's temper. She jumped up, eyes flashing, and snatched her coat from the back of her chair. "You're going to have to come to your senses, Faber," she fumed, jamming her arms into her coatsleeves. "Once and for all." Reserve and any attempt to cover up her true feelings were gone. "Your kind wasn't meant to own land!" she shouted.

Willow sucked in a sharp breath at the ugly words. A cold shiver raced down her spine, she felt sick, then hotly angry. This once, *she* had something to say to Miss Auberta Steele. "Maybe, ma'am, you don't know our kind very well." Willow was on her feet. "We're proud folk, you see. We're not afraid of work. We don't give up easy when we set our minds to a thing. Maybe the Fabers are different than you thought?" Willow's heart was beating fast; she was afraid, talking so to a grown-up. But she could not be still. Not after seeing the terrible hurt the spinster's words brought to Mama's face.

"Humph!" Auberta snorted. With her chin leading, she turned and stomped out.

The lengthy silence following Auberta Steele's abrupt leave-taking was broken after a moment by Papa's soft moan. "Oh, our neighbor is angry with us, *yah*."

"Well, Papa," Jessamyn blurted, "she's not a very nice neighbor." Her chin quivered, her pretty face rosy from humiliation. Willow turned from Jessy toward her mother and saw that Mama's face was hidden behind her lifted apron. Poor Mama, that was the worst of all. When the apron came down, there were tears flooding from Mama's eyes. Her voice was small, childlike, "Why she say, *our kin'?*"

Willow was at her side in a second. "Mama, don't, don't even think about it." Her arm went around her mother, drawing Mama, shivering, against her. "Those dumb, stupid words don't mean anything, not to anybody with good sense."

"I hear the same words other times, in past. Never bother me so much before," Mama whispered. "We try so hard. We no hurt anybody; we work so hard. *Mon Dieu*, you no think person would talk bad like that to us."

"That's exactly why you can't pay any attention to what that selfish, greedy, old witch said," Willow urged. "Look around you, Mama, look. I don't see anybody here who isn't any good! That little baby asleep in her basket, not waking even with all this fuss? Papa, always decent to everybody, even Auberta Steele? Jessy, who could be a princess, anywhere, but who cooks and cleans and never hardly ever complains? Walsh, who works himself ragged trying to keep up and be as good as Papa? Adan and little Laurel, still working over there trying to crack those impossible black walnuts? Clay—and Clay . . . oh, my . . ." Willow sputtered to sudden silence.

Until now, nobody had noticed that Clay was standing on the table. He squatted to pick up the jar of nutmeats, shaking it, a big grin almost overwhelming his small face. "When I grow up," he said chortling, "and get a farm for me, I gonna get Auberta Steele for my hired man. She a good worker!"

There was an instant's silence, then the laughter started, a choked gasp, a soft rumble, then a rollicking roar from all of them together, filling the room.

All the while she laughed along with the others, a deep-down feeling of pride and love for her family was growing stronger inside Willow. Who could stop them? Who'd dare try?

Two days before Christmas, Willow looked out the kitchen window and saw Frank Tucker riding Belle through their gate. Behind the horse, tied with a rope, he dragged a small cedar tree. Willow threw on a coat and went out to help him put Belle in the barn and bring the fragrant tree onto the porch. "Found it over on Johncreek while I was checking my traps," he told her, his breath making little white puffs in the frigid air. "Thought it'd make a perfect Christmas tree."

"C'mon, inside," Willow invited, first stamping her feet on the porch step to free the wet clinging snow from her shoes. Mama's warm kitchen smelled deliciously of cinnamon and ginger when they went in. Willow soon gathered that Frank had more on his mind than the ginger cookies he set to gobbling almost faster than Mama could take them from the oven.

Suddenly, he blurted, "Mrs. Faber, I got a turkey. My uncles want me to cook it for our Christmas dinner, but I don't know how. Do you reckon if I brought it here for you to cook, Uncle Eliot and Uncle Egbert and me could join you folks for Christmas dinner?"

Now that his mind was unburdened of its mission, Frank's face took on a look of vast relief. Willow suppressed a smile when Mama hugged him. "*Bien, bien,*" Mama said, "the turkey you bring him to me. You come to Christmas dinner, yes, and the uncles, too."

Frank sighed. "It's an awful big turkey. If there is anyone else you want to invite—?"

"Doretta and her mother," Willow said promptly, and the others nodded in agreement.

On Christmas Eve, Frank Tucker and Doretta came by to help the Faber children string popcorn and decorate the cedar tree. Doretta brought a small bag of sugar that she had colored red with plum juice. She showed the Fabers how to dip dried apple slices in the red sugar, then pinch and pull the slices into the shape of tiny animals, which they hung on the tree along with the snowy chains of popcorn. Mama sang a Christmas carol for them in French, then Papa took his turn singing a carol in Swedish.

All in all, it was a good Christmas, Willow reflected Christmas night, after the Lawrences and Abrahams had gone and she was in bed. Mama's delicious dinner had left them all moaning with regret that they had eaten so much. Yet each of them found room for an orange from the bag that was Doretta and her mother's gift. On top of that was a huge red-beribboned box of bakery sweets from the Baxters.

Willow grinned into the dark. Did Jessamyn know she had seen Farley give her a small gift, separate from the bakery goodies? Standing near a window in the far corner of the front room, Jessamyn had gasped in delight when she opened the tiny mirrored compact filled with perfumed face powder. Farley looked like a happy little rooster, seeing Jessy's pleasure. Mama wouldn't allow a twelve-year-old to use the powder, Willow was sure, but she also had little doubt that her sister would treasure it every second until she could. She was glad Jessamyn had gotten a special gift. The presents Jessy had made in her bedroom "factory"—stuffed toys, puzzles and paperdolls, sachets, embroidered hankies and scarves, and even a skin pouch for Papa's pipe tobacco—had done a lot to make the rest of the family happy today.

In the middle of that night, Willow woke suddenly, her body stiffened with a feeling of concern. She lay still for a few seconds, wondering if it was the rosebush nightmare that had caused her to wake up. Her face was very cold, and she lifted her hands to warm her cheeks. Then, she heard it, Mama's chickens raising cain. Something terrible was happening out in the new chicken house Papa'd built. Willow leaped from bed. She raced through the house, other family members coming fast on her heels.

All in their nightclothes, they crowded close to Willow when she opened the back door. Everything sparkled outside—frost on the ground, stars in the night sky. "There, Papa!" Walsh yelped, "see, running from the chicken house? There he goes past the barn; ain't carrying anything. It—it's a weasel, yeah, a white weasel!"

"An ermine," Jessamyn corrected as they closed the door to keep from freezing. "Wasn't he pretty?"

"Pretty? *Mon Dieu!* He probably ate half my chickens, he is pretty?" Mama cried, flapping about the kitchen, lighting lamps, bumping into chairs and looking not unlike one of her own worrying hens.

"We'll see, Mama, maybe not," Willow tried to console her. She and Papa dressed and went out to the chicken house, Papa carrying a lantern, to see what harm was done. The chickens were still unsettled, their squawking was ear-piercing yet.

"There ladies," Papa crooned to quiet them, "is all right. *Yah*, sure. You not hurt now."

"There's only one," Willow said, lifting the dead bloodied hen for Papa to see. "The weasel must have dropped it in his hurry. See, there's where he dug his way inside." Willow pointed to a corner where she'd spotted a small mound of fresh-churned dirt just inside the wall.

Papa shook his head and frowned. "We clean hen, Mama can cook it for dinner tomorrow. Is bad. She not like. Mama wants her good laying hens for eggs to sell."

"There's no help for it, Papa, except to fix the hole and hope the weasel doesn't come back. The hen is dead."

Shivering, Willow crawled back into her blankets a short while later. She was drowsily close to sleep when she heard an odd hissing sound—coming from the next room, the boys' lean-to bedroom. She listened. Walsh and Adan, whispering. More than a little annoyed, Willow threw back her quilt and stepped out onto the icy floor. How could anybody sleep? She'd give those two a shaking that'd make their heads rattle! Wide awake now, Willow could make out their words and she stopped short.

"Ermines," Walsh whispered hoarsely, "them white weasels, is worth a fortune. Big city women just lose their minds for ermineskin coats. Adan, we got to get that white weasel for Willow."

"She's out of her mind for a fur coat?" Adan sounded doubtful. "It don't seem like Willow'd want that. How about a saddle, or—"

"Shut up a minute, Adan, an' listen. Not for a coat for her. For money. The money she could get for the ermine skin, to put with the yellow crock savins'. 'Member them two traps in the barn? Rusty. But they'll work. Tomorrow, we start trapping."

"Shoot," Adan whined, "why we got to give our fortune to Willow, anyhow? I been wantin' that Daisy air rifle in the Sears catalogue all my life, and the—"

"Listen," Walsh interrupted. "Ol' Whip's been plenty mean to us. But we oughta remember that she wants The Ranch for all us Fabers, and she's worked harder than anybody to get it for us."

Adan's sigh was long and filled with regret. "Awright. But when I find that treasure in the grove, it's gonna be mine. *All* mine. When it gets warm, when it's spring, I'm gonna dig everything up all over again."

Willow bit her lip to keep from saying anything and crept back to her bed with a good, warm feeling inside. The rascals. They wanted to help her. Of course, digging for imaginary gold coins, or trapping for a sneak-thief weasel wasn't the way. Or was it? Trapping might be. . . .

Willow lay in the dark with her hands clasped behind her head, thinking. On every rented farm where they'd lived, she'd known of neighbor boys who trapped for spending money. The idea of killing little animals and taking their hides to sell had always made her sick, so she never had trapped and she'd managed till now to talk Walsh out of it.

But could she maybe get used to it? Walsh was right when he said ermine skins were valuable. Did she have a right to be soft over wild things when, with a little toughness, she could add plenty of cash to the money in the yellow crock?

Next time she saw Frank, Willow made up her mind, she would ask him about trapping. How to go about it, where they might sell the skins, everything.

eleven

ILLOW was just finishing the milking in the cold, dusky barn that smelled of cows and summer-cut hay, when Frank appeared a few nights later.

"There's not a lot to it," he said, in answer to her questions about trapping. "I take my pelts to Mr. Gill, at the wagon works in Seena. He sells them to a man from Topeka, who pays good. Muskrat are thick along the banks of Johncreek, and along other cricks in these parts. There are some beaver, ermine, too."

"I want to know about the traps. How do you set them, and where?"

Frank hunkered down, grabbed a milking stool, and sat on it. "You look for tracks, first, and muskrat dens. Muskrat leave a plain trail," he told her, "and they make their dens in crick banks. You put your trap close to the crick bank just under the water. You cover the trap with stuff muskrat like to eat— fresh water clams, roots, or twigs. The trap is chained to a stake that you drive into the creek bottom, out in deeper water."

"Wh-what happens to the muskrat, when it's trapped?" Willow asked, picking up a piece of straw and studying it closely.

Frank drew a long breath. "Well, once a muskrat, or mink, is caught in a trap—he fights. That throws him, trap and all, into the water. The stake keeps him from getting back to land and he drowns."

Willow could feel the blood run from her face. She sat down quickly in the straw at her feet. "I—I wish I hadn't asked."

"What's wrong?" Frank wanted to know. "Does it bother you that much? You don't have to do it."

Willow looked up, glared at Frank. "That's what you say! You, with two rich old uncles." Willow was immediately sorry. "I shouldn't have lost my temper. I'm sorry I said that, Frank. But you're wrong. I have to trap whether I like it or not, if it will help us buy The Ranch that much sooner."

The spark of return anger showing in Frank's eyes lessened. After a moment he said quietly, "Maybe you'll get used to it. Remind yourself of the damage those varmints do to your crops in the summertime. Remember the weasel, after your Mama's chickens. That should do it. Anyway, if you want to go ahead with it, we have lots of traps at our place." He looked down and trailed a stick he picked up through the straw on the barn floor. Then he looked up again at Willow. "Some of the traps are rusty, and a lot are broken, but we can fix you a good string. The more traps you set, the more pelts you'll have to sell. You can do real good. If you're sure, want to start tomorrow?"

Willow looked at Frank and tried to ignore the ferocious pounding of her heart, the sick feeling at the pit of her stomach. She nodded. "Let's go ahead with it. Tomorrow."

Next day, their quiet breathing, crunching footsteps, and the *clank clank* of their traps sounded eerie in the stillness as they hiked along. Now and then, naked tree branches rubbed together causing an odd creaking above their heads. Willow drew in her breath when Frank halted to show her the muskrat tracks in the thin crust of white that covered the ground. The five-fingered prints looked for all the world, Willow thought, like they had been made by tiny human hands. Looking down at the tracks, so simple to follow, she again had feelings of doubt and guilt. She squelched them as well as she could.

They set over a dozen traps the first day, and in less than a week half the traps held results. It was cold, ugly work, removing the small sodden bodies of muskrat from the traps. But Willow kept at it, each day after school. Evenings, after supper, Frank came and helped her skin her catch. "I'm not getting used to it," she mumbled one evening, staring at her bloody hands and shaking her head. "I'm not getting used to it one bit—it's worse all the time." Her voice sounded flat even to her own ears. A heaviness settled under her breast bone.

"I could do the skinning alone, if that's what bothers you?" Frank offered, in the form of a question.

"All of it bothers me," Willow said, her voice still a leaden whisper. "It seems so mean, Frank. It's so unfair. The poor little critters aren't really hurting much, just taking a little corn or grain here and there. Going about their business of living on this earth, their way, same as the rest of us."

"Quit. Give it up, you better," Frank insisted. "I—I don't like it—seeing it bother you this much. Do something else."

"I—I can't," Willow answered in a choked growl from trying to cover up the crying feeling inside her. She didn't want to start crying in front of Frank. She hardly ever cried anymore. Why now? She swallowed, got herself in hand. "Tomorrow, tomorrow or the next day, or the next, I could have a mink or a beaver in one of my traps. I can't take a chance on losing out on something that valuable."

Frank shrugged helplessly. "All right. Suit yourself, Wil'."

Willow gave him a tiny smile. "Thanks, Frank. I—I'm glad you're helping me."

A LEAD gray sky told of impending snow late one afternoon when Willow finished checking her trapline at the picnic grove pond. She'd gotten Walsh and Adan to check her traps on Johncreek. As she hurried to meet her brothers there, a few flakes of snow drifted down, biting her numb face. Willow traveled southwest along Johncreek. About a mile past the schoolhouse she spotted the round, bundled figures of her brothers trudging along through the trees ahead. Willow opened her mouth to call to Walsh and Adan, changed her mind, and ran to catch up instead.

"How—how are you doing?" she panted when she reached them.

"Not as g-good as y-you." Walsh spoke through chattering teeth. His glance covered the two musk-rat and one mink that bobbed lifeless from her belt.

Willow saw that Walsh's lips were almost blue. Adan stood hunched and silent, with only his eyes showing above the gray wool scarf wound up over his cap and around his face. "Let's check a few more traps, then we'll go home and get warm," Willow told them.

Later, as they drew close to the last trap on their line, Willow halted and with her arms outstretched stopped her brothers behind her. "I think—I hear something. Did you hear a—a *baby* crying?" she whispered.

"Out here?" Walsh's attempt at laughter came out a thin gurgle through his chilled lips. "Ain't gonna be no baby down here by the crick." He pulled away from Willow's arm and stumbled on. "I'm not gonna stand here and freeze."

"Walsh, wait!" Willow ordered, going around him again to take the lead. The whimpering sound was plain as they arrived at the place where they'd set the last trap. A soft splashing could be heard down over the bank. Willow looked, closed her eyes, and looked again. The mother beaver's struggles were feeble against the trap that held her. Her sleek brown baby paddled alongside in the water, whimpering piteously.

Willow reeled away from the sight, her arms clutched tight across her stomach. "What've we done?" Her voice was hollow with shock. "Oh, what've we done." She stumbled to a nearby tree—and was sick.

Walsh muttered, "Jeez." In another minute he yelled, "*Wait, Willow!* Hey, what we gonna do?"

Only then did Willow understand that she was running hard away. The awful feelings inside—the guilt, the sickness, churned as she ran. She couldn't, couldn't stand it—had to get away, away from feeling like this, had to!

The poor beavers, the poor beavers. Willow's accusing thoughts tormented, urging her along faster and faster, away from what she had done but couldn't escape. Poor beavers. She unfastened the heavy belt at her waist and let it drop without slowing.

Her chest started to ache, her legs were becoming solid pain, and still Willow ran, faster, faster. Scarcely aware of it, Willow reached the blind lane that led toward home. It was snowing in earnest now, the flakes biting tingles on her cheeks.

The wind keened in Willow's ears, the snow

blew hard, as she neared The Ranch. However desperate, her movements were becoming like those of a wound-down robot.

Willow reached her own back porch. She stumbled, fell headlong, then reached for the doorknob and pulled herself up. Without a word, she rushed by Mama cooking at the stove, by the little ones in the kitchen, Jessy. In the back bedroom, she somehow managed to get out of her cold, stiff outer garments. All the while, in her mind, the mother beaver struggled and the baby beaver cried.

"What you do in there?" Mama asked through the closed door. "Something is wrong, eh?"

Willow didn't know what she said, her reply through her numb, chilled lips was a mumble. It must have satisfied Mama, she walked away humming a tune.

For a long time after that, Willow lay on her bed, guilt a continuing sickness in the back of her throat. Trapping was out. She never should have started it. No matter how much it might have helped The Ranch savings. It wasn't possible for her to go against her true feelings about trapping helpless little animals. She hated it, oh, how she hated what she had done. Willow rolled over on the bed, rolled back again.

If only she could undo it, bring life again to the mother beaver, turn the mother back with the baby beaver so its terrible crying would stop. Willow sat up suddenly. The mother wasn't dead, although it had been close to it. Maybe there was time? Had Walsh thought to let it go? Or, had he used a club and. . . . Willow was off the bed and back into her coat and boots in seconds.

She raced through the house, hearing Mama cry, "Willow, where are boys? Where you go? You must help Papa with chores!"

She didn't answer, there wasn't time. Outside, Willow was stunned to see a blinding wall of white. The snowstorm was much worse! The boys were still out in it. They could get lost. Willow glanced over her shoulder and took her bearings from the tall, ghost house and set out west. She would meet the boys coming home probably.

Staying close to the fence, Willow followed the blind lane. She pulled her cap away from her ear so she could hear any sound the boys might make, coming home. As she traveled, the wind died down. There was nothing but deathlike silence in the falling snow. Where were they? "Walsh," she called, "A—dan." They were probably near frozen by now. They were so cold already when she'd caught up to them near the end of the trapline.

"Walsh," she yelled again. "Adan! Please answer me!"

Although there was no one to hear her but herself, Willow couldn't help whispering out loud, "Keeping moving, Walsh. Don't stop to rest, Adan.

You won't freeze, boys, if you keep moving." Wasn't she ever going to find them? While she searched, the time sped on toward dark.

"I've got to find them while there is still daylight, and I will," Willow repeated to herself, trying to put an end to the growing doubt that nagged at her.

Willow had long since turned off the blind lane and now she continued west in the direction of Johncreek. The snow fell like a torrent of goose feathers from the sky. On and on she plodded, letting instinct guide her. She reached the spot where they had caught the mother beaver, and she experienced feelings of both sadness and relief. There was no sign of the trap, nor of the beavers. She couldn't even find a trace of her brothers' footsteps in the thickening white on the ground, though she could recognize the tree where she'd been sick.

Fear took a hard grip on Willow. Which way had the boys gone? They didn't take the right direction for home or she would have met them. "Walsh!" she screamed suddenly, "Adan!" Willow listened with every bit of her being for an answer. There was no sound except the wind, whipping up to a whine, again. *This was her fault, the boys being lost.* Willow swallowed back a sob.

For sure, Walsh and Adan had taken a wrong direction trying to find their way home. But which direction? Willow swiped at her eyes with a frosted mitten and drew herself up. She had to think this out, not continue in a blind tizzy. The boys wouldn't have gone farther west because that way they would have had to cross Johncreek and they would know that was wrong. If they walked north, they ought to have come to the Johncreek Schoolhouse. Or the houses and streets of Seena. And if they had, they would have found their way home easily from there. They hadn't gone east or they'd have met her. At least they ought to have been within hearing distance of her yelling at them.

South, then. It was such a big area, though, wide open fields, with maybe one or two brushy gullies. She couldn't cover every step of it. She could only hope they'd gotten turned around and had taken a direct path south from the spot where they'd caught the beaver.

From time to time as she plunged along, Willow danced a frantic jig to keep her blood from freezing in her veins. She peeled off her mittens and sucked her fingers to bring the circulation back to the numb stubs.

One minute it was daylight, the next it was night. She'd never find them now, Willow thought, in the dark. Her feet, almost with minds of their own, plodded on. Every now and then, she stopped to shout her brothers' names, but the snowy night gave back no answer.

Willow felt like a person dead, a ghost. But she couldn't stop. Couldn't stop.

Much later, Willow stumbled into a clump of

stunted trees. She was thrashing about, trying to find her way through the gnarled, viney trunks, when she thought she heard a sound. Willow stopped, close to fainting, so desperately did she want to bring back the sound to her ears. It came again, then, a soft mewing like that of a lost kitten. With an enormous lunge, Willow headed for the noise and fell across the huddled figures of Walsh and Adan. She struggled to her knees and clutched her young brothers, too overcome with relief to speak.

Willow regained her senses at once. "Get up!" she ordered, "move around or you'll freeze to death. Up. Both of you, get up, you hear me?" She pushed and tugged as ferociously as a mother bear trying to protect her endangered cubs.

"We got lost," she heard Walsh mumble. "W-Willow, h-help us."

When still they didn't move, Willow took a moment to run her hands over her snow-covered brothers and discovered that Adan lay in Walsh's arms. "What's wrong with Adan?" she cried.

"Don't know. He won't move."

"Yes, he will," Willow snarled. "He will so move." She grabbed Adan, yanked him to his feet, and began to drag him back and forth. "Help me, Adan," she said, "don't drag your feet *walk*. This is no time to be lazy. No miracle of good fortune is going to come. It has to be you, this time, you. Use your legs. You, too, Walsh, get up and walk. Grab the tail of my coat and hang onto me. Both of you got to walk until you feel warm. Come on, walk!"

When at last Adan moved his legs on his own, Willow asked, "How do you feel?"

"C-c-cold. N-n-numb," Adan managed to tell Willow.

"You're going to be all right," Willow told him firmly, "all three of us are going to be just fine." She gripped Adan with one arm and walked back and forth. She could feel Walsh's mittened hands caught to her coattail. With her teeth, Willow pulled her own mitten from her free hand and searched the pockets of Papa's barn coat. It had been some time since he used this coat, but maybe she could find something in the pockets. Two matches, thankfully, with heads on. Sometimes Papa cut the heads off and used the matches to clean his fingernails. In another pocket, Willow's fingers discovered three lumps that she recognized as pieces of horehound candy.

Almost afraid to ask, Willow said, "Did either one of you still have your dinner pail from school when you stopped here?" If one of them had, she could build a fire with the matches and twigs from the trees, and in a lard-bucket dinner pail she could melt snow. The horehound candy could go into the water to make them a hot, sweet tea to warm and revive them.

"Both our dinner pails are here, somewhere," Walsh mumbled.

"Good!" Willow kicked about until she located them. "Hang on to one another and keep walking and stay close to my voice," she ordered her brothers. She pried the lid from the first pail with her fingernails and felt inside. "Paper! That'll help start the fire," she told them. "Bread crusts. That will go good with the hot tea I'm going to fix you boys."

"That paper's my arithmetic test," Walsh said, "but I'm glad you're burning it, I got a *D*."

Desperate, worried as she was, Willow managed a laugh through numb lips. "Follow me," she said, "I'll keep talking while I break off some twigs and limbs to build a fire with. Adan, don't you slow down. Walsh, you make him stay with you." A while later, Willow scooped a hollow in the snow and stacked the twigs with Walsh's test paper. "I won't tell Mama about your bad grade," she said as she struck a match to the paper, "but you better, Walsh."

A thankful sob sounded from Adan when the tiny red flame caught and grew. Hunched over with his mittened hands on his knees, he came to the fire reverently. "Go ahead and hold your hands over it," Willow told him, "get your hands warm. Wiggle your toes inside your boots as much as you can. You're going to be all right."

After each of them had a few sips of the hot horehound tea, Walsh asked, "Can we go home now? I feel lots better."

Willow had been dreading this question, and she

took a moment to form her answer. "Boys, I don't know exactly where we are. Even if I made a torch from one of these tree limbs, it's snowing too hard for us to—to find our way home. We could get awful mixed up. There's miles of empty fields around here to get lost in. Think about it, this is a pretty good shelter and there's enough wood to keep our fire going. We'll be better off if we stay where we are." She thought to add quickly, so they wouldn't be too scared, "But first thing come daylight, we'll head home."

"Maybe Papa will find us," Adan suggested hopefully.

"If he doesn't get lost himself looking for us," Willow worried. "I hope he will trust me to take care of you and get you home safe."

Willow built up the fire until it crackled and blazed. "You can sit down to rest, close to the fire, now," she told her brothers, "but only for a little while, then you got to move around again."

Move around, move around, move around. Willow cajoled, begged, bullied, and threatened through the long cold hours. At one point in the night, as they stopped walking to take a few minutes rest by the fire, Willow gathered her nerve to ask, "Walsh, what happened to—to the beavers?"

Although sleepy-eyed, her brother took on a look of remembering, as he studied her face across the rosy flames of the campfire. He said, "We got the mother out of the trap. She was still alive. We wouldn't have been late, we would'a got home before the snow got so bad, only we stayed to watch the beavers, to make sure they were all right."

"And?"

"After a long time, the big mama beaver took her baby off into some brush down at the edge of the water."

"I—I'm so glad, Walsh. I—I . . . thanks an awful lot."

The misery-filled snowy night passed like ten for Willow. Time after endless time she forced herself awake to pile more limbs on the fire and make the boys get up and walk with her.

Scarcely daring to believe her own eyes, Willow sat Indian-fashion, huddling as she watched the eastern sky lighten at last and gradually turn pink. It was over. The awful night was over. Willow got to her feet clumsily, stretched, and rubbed her sore eyes. Everywhere she looked the world was white. But the storm was over for now. Far to the north she could see smoke lifting from many chimneys in Seena. Beautiful sign of life!

Willow looked down at Walsh and Adan huddled together in the deep snow beside their dying fire. Before last night they had so many times called her mean, a whip. If she hadn't deserved the name before, last night she earned it for dead certain. But they were alive. She'd do it again if she had to. Willow reached down and jiggled her brothers' shoulders in turn. "Wake up. We can go home now."

twelve

OWN with bad colds, suffering the pain of frostbitten faces, Willow, Walsh, and Adan, missed the next two weeks of school. As bad as she felt, aching and coughing, Willow was suffering more from guilt that Papa must do everything. His own chores, hers, Walsh's.

"You could have frozen stiff to death," Mama scolded roundly, all the while she smothered them with care. "Your Papa, he come home near to go crazy that night. He afraid they not find his chil'ren's bones till spring." Mama's tongue was razor sharp, a complete contrast to the look in her eyes.

"We are real, real sorry," Willow couldn't repeat enough. "It wasn't fair, worrying you and Papa like that. I'm old enough to know better. It was my fault. Stupid."

Gentle Papa was even angrier, more upset than Mama. "You trap no more, girl. Ranch or no Ranch!"

At that, Willow's throat dried up and she could only nod. There were no words to tell how horrible trapping was to her. There were no shortcuts to getting The Ranch. Hard work was the only way.

When February came, Willow remembered that

this used to be the month Papa went looking for a new farm to rent, went looking for something better for his family. They had found their something better. Here they were on The Ranch with no intention of moving on, ever. Had she honestly believed they had a chance, that it would happen, when she made that wish on a star way back last spring?

A small stab of unease disrupted Willow's feelings of satisfaction, contentment. They hadn't been able to make the down payment on The Ranch, there were no legal papers, yet. Auberta Steele, like a buzzard watching a lamb, was just watching and waiting for some sign of failure on their part.

Lucky for them, in a few short weeks they'd be plowing, putting in their second spring's crops on The Ranch. It had to be a good season, good crops, Willow determined. From now on, they had to get all they could out of each and every day, every piece of work.

Holding true to her vow, Willow threw herself into work, harder than ever, afternoons and weekends, helping Papa. They cleared the grove behind the house of choking brush. They chopped down the oldest dead and diseased trees to season for next year's firewood and to give the other, living, trees a better chance.

To Papa, trees were almost like people. "We take care of our trees," he told Willow, caressing the silvery trunk of a cottonwood, "they take care of us. *Yah*. This grove cuts wind, gives shelter. Makes shade for our house in summer. Give us firewood, now." He grew more thoughtful. "Trees grow plenty in Sweden, not like Kansas with so few. Ay, sometime I miss my old homelands's big green trees."

Willow could have added her own thoughts about the grove. She agreed with Papa's beliefs, but on the other hand, the shady grove was a hideout from work for Adan, Laurel, and Clay. Looking for treasure most of last summer! Frittering away valuable time. She hoped they wouldn't give her so much trouble this spring. *Willow whip* they called her. All right, she'd make them get up and get if she had to. What was the sense to mollycoddling them when there was so much work to be done?

In March, Willow and Papa spread manure from the barns—"dressing" Papa called it—on their fields. Willow felt a glow of satisfaction, looking out on the ribbons of valuable fertilizer crossing the snow-white fields. Along with the melting snow, it would soak into the ground, making their fields richer.

As the days passed, it became harder and harder to feel happy about leaving The Ranch to attend school. Willow found the overheated classrooms too stuffy, too noisy; it was next to impossible to concentrate on her studies. The boys and girls around her, even the teachers, began to seem a touch silly, fribble-heads, most of them.

How come she had ever thought school friends were so important? Willow was thinking one day. And the parties, plays and programs, school paper, and pretty soon now, those silly slow baseball games that wasted so much time? You couldn't have your cake and eat it too, she'd found.

It was different for many of the kids in her room. Somebody had made their place for them. From the moment they were born it was ready. Mama and Papa hadn't been able to do that for her, not to fault them. They had a chance now, with her helping. In time, the Fabers would count. But there wasn't time, just yet, to have the trimmings on life like these others could have now.

That same afternoon after school, Willow headed down the hall feeling in a special hurry to get home to The Ranch. She and Papa were almost finished dressing the fields. Maybe they'd finish today, there would be a few hours daylight, yet. Deep in thought, Willow jumped when someone caught her elbow, coming up from behind. Her heart thumped.

"Whoa, funny friend," Frank said, using her name for him. "Slow down. I didn't hear the fire bell."

Willow took a moment to catch her breath, for her pounding heart to come back to normal. Then she turned on a heel toward him, rolling her eyes, "Look, Frank," she warned, "you know better than anybody that I got a lot to do at home. What do you want?"

He explained fast, "My uncles' birthdays are this Friday. I thought I might have some of the neighbors come over, right after school. Have two birthday cakes." There was a sense of excitement, fun, dancing in the blue eyes looking down at her. "Two kinds of ice cream, hats for them, you know. Could you help me with it?"

Willow felt a weakening inside. A birthday party for two old men, twins, it'd be different. Fun. And nobody had been so good to them as Egbert and Eliot Abraham. Willow stood on one foot, then the other, torn with indecision. She let out a long sigh. If she and Papa finished dressing the fields today, they could begin plowing Friday—the fields they'd dressed first. She looked down, saying nothing.

"You—you're too busy." Frank's voice was flat, accusing.

"I'm glad you see—you understand, how it is," Willow spoke quietly, moving to pass him.

Frank stepped out of her way, then seemed to suddenly change his mind. He caught Willow's shoulders in his hands and held her tight, made her look up at him. "I know it's gonna cause the world to come to an end, as far as you're concerned," his young voice stung, "but waste one second listening to me." The blue eyes looking at her were a storm of hurt and caring. "I like you, Willow; I like you so much I have to tell you you're headin' for trouble. You're gonna have a headful of gray hair before you're—you're fifteen. You're going to be as swaybacked as your old mule, Jen, if you don't smarten' up."

A terrible pain seemed to crush something inside Willow. "Smarten' up?" she gasped. "You mean be lazy, don't you? Fool around?" she snapped. "Waste time? Be the good-for-nothing I'm *supposed* to be?"

He shook his head quickly, "Not that. I—I mean, please take some time for something besides work. Help me with the party?"

At that worst possible moment, Willow saw Jarma Walbridge and Melinda Lewis coming upon them in the hallway; they'd heard most every word between her and Frank, probably. Willow opened her mouth to say something, but blonde Melinda, who looked perfect in a red sweater and plaid skirt, said very loud, "Why would any one bother with Willow Faber? She's got seeds on the brain." She giggled. "And manu-cow droppings on her shoes."

All of them. Against her. Ganging up.

Stout Jarma, in dull forest green, added, "Frank, ask Willow which she likes best, and I'll bet she'll choose corn and pigs over having any fun with the rest of us kids."

It was cruel and ugly put like that. But it was still the truth, and it hit home. Fighting tears of rage, Willow gave the giggling girls a look meant to kill. She wrestled from Frank's sturdy arms trying to comfort her, and ran. *Damn the damfool cussed lot of them!* Willow stormed silently, as she flew down the hall, *Frank Tucker, too.* She hoped she never saw him again, ever, her entire lifetime!

As she ran toward home, Willow stayed so angry she was hardly aware of where she was going or why. *Ignoramuses!* a voice inside her screamed silently. *Blind, hee-hawing donkeys, all of them. Without the sense to come in out of the rain. They couldn't see!*

She would show them. The gigantic wave of fury gripped Willow until bedtime. Then, she lay with her hot face pushed deep into her pillow, her head spinning, her eyes dry and aching. What the others didn't seem to know was that a person had to give everything for what they wanted. Or why want it at all? They had the nerve to make out that she was the one who was wrong!

She knew she was doing the right thing. But, why, then, did she feel this rotten, hateful way inside? How come, deep down, did she feel so sorry about missing Frank's uncles' birthday?

What was she supposed to do? She couldn't be two people. By now, Frank had probably asked Melinda and Jarma to help him. Was it important, something she shouldn't miss? Was this tangle of troubles her doing? Was she wrong?

Aching for sleep and relief from her worries, too tired to shed tears, Willow closed her burning eyes. In time, she slept.

As well as weekends, Willow began to spend two or three days each week, at home. The few days she attended school, if Frank looked at her at all, his expression told her nothing. The others were no different than usual. Sometimes, she felt bothered by the break with Frank, as well as missing out on the good times at school. If only the days weren't so full of things to be done. No matter, she couldn't be selfish, take time for herself to frolic, be like the others at school.

Mama plainly didn't like Willow staying home weekdays, but she kept it to herself. Papa allowed it because he did need her. In the past weeks the last trace of snow had melted, leaving the barnyard a foot-deep quagmire of mud. Day after day, the sun poured down, drying the earth. Out in the fields, the black dirt steamed, became friable, begged to be turned.

Jen pulled Papa's walking plow. Papa, his hands gripped to the plow handles, the lines over his shoulders, stumbled along after, making the rows of shiny-black, curled earth arrow straight. With Ben hitched to the harrow, Willow soon followed, turning to a soft crumble the fields Papa'd plowed earlier. Then, the planting.

The seed was scarcely in the ground, it seemed, before their fields were sprouting new green. Willow watched the wheat field she had planted the previous fall with growing horror. The wheat came up in miserable, scraggly patches, like hair on a dog balding with mange. For sure she'd done something wrong, or there was something wrong with the seed she had used. That was when Papa was hurt; she'd finished the planting alone. Maybe she planted too deep.

"Our wheat crop not be good," Papa agreed in deep solemnity, surveying the field one day with Willow. "We be lucky if we get enough seed from that field just for ourselves."

"You don't think we'll get any to sell? The Ranch, the down payment, Papa, what'll we do?" Willow asked. When Papa didn't answer right away she set to pacing back and forth at the edge of the sorry-looking field, hands in her pockets. Finally, she came to a halt behind him. "Papa, please tell me, is there anything we can do?"

Deep lines were etched in Papa's face, when he turned and he took a still longer time to answer. "We forget wheat," he told her at last, "hope alfalfa is good crop and will make up for loss. We got more ground planted to alfalfa than anything else. We get two, three cuttings from it. We will sell first cuttings, save later ones for ourselves. Making hay is hard work," he added. "You remember, daughter. And it will be harder this year with so much alfalfa hay to put up. But alfalfa can make down payment."

Willow looked at him, gave a deep sigh. "We can do the work, Papa. You don't have to worry about that."

"Not alone," Papa told her, shaking his head. "Is too hard. We get help. Maybe hire two or three soldiers to help us. Since Germans surrender, the soldiers come home faster to America, more of them every month. I hear Seena's doctor, a man named Matthews, is finally home from war. But so many have no job, they just sit around in town, loafing. I think they rather have work, *yah*."

Willow still had a question. "Papa," she asked, gnawing at her bottom lip, "do you think we can earn enough off our alfalfa to make the down payment on The Ranch and pay wages to a hay crew, besides?"

Papa squinted, looking at her, an eyebrow lifted, but he was smiling around his corncob pipe. "Ay think so, *yah*. We see, don't we, business-lady?"

Her return grin was feeble. Willow drew her shoulders up. "All right, Papa, if you think so. Nothing we can do but try, it's our last chance."

A few days later, Willow's hoe flashed in the dazzling spring sunshine as she attacked the new sunflower weeds trying to come up in this year's corn crop. Out of the corner of her eye, Willow saw a movement that made her stop hoeing to look.

A tiny figure moved across the far east corner of the horse pasture. "Clay, you little tramp," she shouted with her hand cupped around her mouth, "you get back to the house!" He hesitated, looking in Willow's direction. If she had to stop work and go to the house to tell them to keep Clay in the yard . . . ! Willow's pulse hammered at her temple, she motioned with her hoe toward the house. Finally,

Clay turned and trudged back the way he had come. Willow returned to her hoeing with a tired grunt of irritation.

Four-year-old Clay, always daring and curious, had taken to wandering this spring, near his fifth birthday. And it was becoming a trial to go looking for him when he got lost. Willow had warned Clay time and again, "Stay out of the pasture, away from those big horses, or you're apt to get kicked silly, if not dead." She was sure it went in one ear and out the other. Willow looked up now, to see if Clay was any nearer the house. With a sigh of relief, she saw that he was back playing in a dirt pile in the yard with Mitty—she could see their cottony heads.

When Willow went into noon dinner, she complained to Mama about Clay being in the pasture. "I can't work and watch him, too," she insisted. "Somebody here at the house better keep track of him."

Mama shook her head, her eyes worried. "What to do, I don't know. One minute he with me helping clean henhouse. Or with Jessy weeding garden. Next minute—*voilà*, he no to be seen." Mama shook her spoon at Clay, eating unconcernedly, his face close to his plate of snap beans and bacon. "You get hurt bad sometime," she warned him, "and we not be there to help you. You stay close to house like good boy."

Finished with her meal, Willow shoved back from the table and stood up, wiping a drop of milk from her chin with the back of her hand. "He needs a whipping, Mama, one good hard whipping. That'd keep him home." She headed for the door, but not so soon that she didn't see the flare of anger in Mama's eyes.

"You no tell me how to bring up my young ones, *ma chérie*," Mama said quietly, "they my babies, not yours."

"Then keep him home!" Willow shouted at Mama in weary exasperation. She yanked the door open. "I got work to do. I can't go chasing off looking for him every half-hour."

Until now, Papa hadn't spoken, nor moved. But Willow wasn't two steps down the back porch when he caught up to her and grabbed her shoulder. Papa turned her toward him. "You don't talk that way to your mama, daughter. *Nay*," he said sternly. "Maybe you need little slap, yourself?"

Willow didn't meet Papa's eyes. Feeling flushed, angry, tormented, she waited silently, listening to Papa's hard breathing. He said, "I go to Abrahams this afternoon to see if they got part I need for cultivator. I want no more trouble at home while I'm gone," Papa warned. When he didn't say anything more for some seconds, Willow turned and headed for the field.

She couldn't for the life of her figure out what people wanted from her! Furious, she snatched up her hoe and went back to work with a vengeance.

The Fabers had two choices: they could earn The Ranch, put down roots right here, or they could be fiddlefoot nobodies the rest of their days. She knew what she wanted. But the rest of them!

Willow trembled. Could she be blamed because wanting The Ranch was like a-a fire inside her? Nobody, nothing, could smother that out, so why didn't everybody stop fighting her, stop giving her so much trouble?

Maybe it was that the rest of the family didn't feel it so strong as she did, didn't want to stay on here as much as she did. Or, maybe they wanted The Ranch only if it was handed to them on a silver platter? That wasn't going to happen! Already, she was doing her part, more than her share. Did she complain about being dog-tired numb around the clock, day in and day out? Never a change?

She could quit. They could go back to the old ways. They could take Auberta Steele's shanty in town for a while, then move, then . . . then . . . then . . . Willow shivered, closed her eyes, shook her head. *No!*

Some things could be easier around here. Mama could be tougher on the young ones, make them help more. That blamed Adan was right back digging in the grove again this spring, spending acres of time looking for treasure that wasn't there, looking for nothing, using time for nothing. Nobody stopped him.

Was she the only one could see that Adan was old enough to drive a team, cultivate, milk cows? Nobody made him do anything.

What was happening around here? Why was everything going wrong? With a feeling close to murder in her heart, Willow lifted her hoe with a *swish* and hacked a tiny pigweed into bits.

thirteen

P USHED along by anger and frustration as much as energy and will, Willow accomplished twice as much as usual that afternoon. She ignored the bad ache that settled in her back, finished hoeing one row of corn and started back on the next. Finally, an edgy feeling that something was wrong brought her glance up, and she saw Jessamyn racing along the row toward her, waving her arms.

Jessy's motions were so frantic, Willow couldn't keep her heart from skipping a beat. But she waited where she was and mopped the sweat from her brow on her sleeve. Her sister was shouting now, muddled words, that Willow finally made out. "Clay," Jessamyn was saying, "it's Clay."

Oh, no, she wouldn't! They had no right to ask her to help find Clay, not after what had happened at noon, Mama and Papa scolding her. Willow ignored Jessy's pleading yells and went back to work; her hoe made a deft arch and came up under a morning glory weed to leave it, roots and all, to die in the sun.

In the next moment Jessy reached her, panting raggedly. She grabbed Willow's arm and said, "Clay's been bit by a rattlesnake. He was in the pasture and—"

Willow went cold all over in spite of the broiling sun. "I warned you. I warned all of you to keep him in the yard," she muttered in dark anger. But her firm intent not to help was gone. She started off in a run toward the house.

"Papa's not come back from the Abrahams'," Jessamyn panted as they ran. "Mama wants you to take Clay in to that doctor that's come back to Seena, Dr. Matthews. It may be—be too late, his foot is swollen twice the size it ought to be, and it's turning black. Walsh is putting the saddle on Eagle for you."

"All right," Willow mumbled, "all right." After what seemed an eternity they reached the barnyard and Willow mounted Eagle on the run. She grabbed a white-faced Clay as Mama passed him up to her, deftly turned Eagle toward the road, and dug in her heels. As they galloped away, west toward Seena, Mama's distraught face stayed etched in Willow's mind.

With Paul Revere-like speed they rode through town and came to a halt in front of the doctor's small white house, which was also his office. With strength she didn't know she had, being so tired, Willow carried Clay up the honeysuckle bordered walk and rapped hard on the door. It opened after a moment, and in a voice harsh with worry, she told the doctor why they were there.

Dr. Matthews, a rotund man in a rumpled suit, listened carefully, then ushered Willow and Clay through his cool, blind-drawn house into a sunny examining room where he motioned for Willow to put Clay on the table. She put Clay down, then walked jerkily to a chair in the corner, feeling weak, her straw hat clasped in her work-begrimed hands.

The doctor examined Clay's foot so slowly, Willow decided Clay would probably die. The doctor ought to be doing something—drawing the poison out, cutting, something! Finally, Dr. Matthews straightened, hooked his thumbs in his vest pockets, and rocked back on his heels, a quizzical look in his eyes. Willow was about to scream her impatience when the doctor spoke, "This boy's foot is badly squashed, not broken, not snakebit."

Willow let the words sink in, for a minute thinking the doctor was crazy. She shook her head, bewildered. "N-not snakebit? They said a snake. . . . *Squashed!*" She was voiceless for a full minute as she tried to figure that out. "Clay," she demanded finally, "was there a snake? Did you see or hear a rattlesnake?"

There was fear written in Clay's fluttering eyelids, his quivering mouth, as he looked at Willow. That was new! Clay began to cry, his shoulders drawn in, and he shook his head.

"No snake? What happened—?" Even before she finished the question, Willow knew the answer. Clay was out in the pasture. "Clay," she was close to yelling, "did one of the horses or mules step on you?"

"Dul-Dulcie d-did." Clay's answer came from far, far away.

"Clay! Why didn't you say so?" Willow lunged toward him, flinging her straw hat into the chair. "Why didn't you tell Mama what happened, really?"

Clay sobbed in earnest, now. "M-Mama looked at my f-foot and—and said I was snakebit prob-probably. I thought maybe—maybe I was."

"You knew better," Willow stormed. "Why didn't you tell Mama the truth, that Dulcie stepped on your foot?"

"She didn't ask me!" Clay wailed. "Nobody asked me did Dulcie step on my foot?" His narrow shoulders shook with sobs.

Willow's face was crimson with embarrassment. It was all she could do to look at the doctor. "Th-thank you for looking at my brother's foot. Next time I come to town I'll bring butter and eggs to pay you. Today—today there wasn't time."

The doctor for some reason turned his back to them; he waved an arm. "Nah," his voice came muffled, "no charge. There isn't much can be done to help the foot, just time. Keep him off of it. S-soak it in epsom salts, warm wa-water." The doctor waved them toward the door. As soon as the door closed after Willow and the limping Clay, Willow heard the doctor's loud *hoo-raw* of laughter burst loose inside the house.

"Durn you, Clay!" Willow muttered, turning

hot from head to foot. "Durn you all to heck."

They rode home in stony silence. Some member of the family must have been stationed to watch for them because when Willow and Clay rode into the yard, all of the others were there, even Papa home from the Abrahams', pacing, watching.

"Clay, he is all right? The doctor fix him?" Mama rushed to take her young son from in front of Willow on the horse. Mama's yellow apron was a wrinkled mess from twisting it in her worry, Willow saw. Mama held the boy close to her and looked at the dark, swollen foot.

"Ask him how he is," Willow grated, dismounting. "Just ask him! Make him tell you exactly what happened."

Slowly, fumblingly, tears flowing, Clay confessed.

"*Non*," Mama said, shaking her head. "You did that? Bad boy, bad boy," she crooned in a voice that made the scolding sound like a song of love.

"Blister his bottom, Mama, that's what he needs!" Willow insisted, pointing. She waited, but Mama didn't spank Clay. "He made me feel like a dumb fool in front of that doctor," Willow went on, shaking her finger at Clay. "I had to leave the field for nothing. Now one of you spank him!" Willow looked from Mama to Papa but neither of them moved. Instead, they stared at her, silent, looking shocked.

Willow took a step toward Clay, "All right,"

she said in a belligerent voice that told of her warlike mood, "I guess I have to do this, too."

Papa blocked her way. "I'm ashamed for you, daughter," he whispered. "We punish Clay, but not like this. His foot is sore, bad hurt, that is punishment. Your mama is happy he isn't snakebitten, can't you see? What is matter with you? Why you act like this? You're not like my daughter, Willow Sabrina. *Nay,* I don't know this girl in front of me."

Willow's face flamed, she clenched her fists. "This is—is the last st-straw," she cried, backing away from her family. "I have to do it all, everything. Nobody will do what I tell them. I'll do everything myself, then. Don't help me, nobody, if that's what you want. Clay can just keep running off. I'll get this Ranch by myself. I will!" Willow could feel them all staring at her back as she whirled and led Eagle to the barn, but silence followed her every step of the way.

The young ones steered wide around Willow for days afterward. They seldom spoke to her directly. Mama and Papa were outwardly polite, but many times Willow was aware that they watched her, were studying her as though there was something about her they couldn't understand, some change that must be corrected if only they could figure it out.

It wasn't her fault. She'd tried to tell them what it was, how she felt about getting The Ranch, overcoming things that stood in the way; and she'd been scolded for it. She wouldn't say another word. She had her work to do. With the family staying away from her, she'd get that much more done.

A few days later when the sun was just going down and one of the cows was lowing for her evening milking, Willow gave up work for the day and trudged wearily from the middle of the corn-patch. She gave a start of surprise when she looked up to see her brothers and sisters racing toward her like water from a broken dam. Only Clay stayed back, at the edge of the field, hopping up and down in one spot. He'd learned his lesson, maybe, or was he, finally, that afraid of her?

"Adan done it!" Walsh, in the lead, shouted, "an' you said he wouldn't. Adan hit treasure!"

Willow didn't bother to remind Walsh that he didn't think Adan would find treasure, either, she was too tired. Besides, this was the unlikeliest story she'd ever heard.

"Come on, Willow, hurry!" Jessy, even, believing it.

"Wait till you see," Laurel piped.

Let *them* run, Willow thought. She followed slowly, her mind beginning to stir. Adan had probably uncovered some junk, like the dog bones. But on the chance that he had found something really valuable . . . their troubles would be over, sooner. They wouldn't have to wait until after haying, maybe, to pay on The Ranch. "Wait up," Willow said finally, in a voice hoarse with fatigue.

She followed the others toward the barn, envisioning, in spite of herself, an ancient, dirt-covered chest overflowing with gold coins and jewels. "What is it?" Willow croaked, her curiosity mounting. "What'd you find, Adan?" There was a proud, confident set to the boy's shoulders as he motioned toward something that lay on a pile of old burlap bags in the shadows by the barn. Willow's spirits dipped low. She couldn't see what it was, but it sure wasn't a chest of gold.

"See." Adan pointed.

"You call that treasure?" Willow snapped. "It's nothing but a rusty old sword." She fought an urge to box all of them on the ears.

Jessamyn, her voice peaked almost to a squeal, said, "Willow, stop being stubborn and mean. You're not even looking. Take a good look at the sword. Remember Coronado?"

Willow looked, remembered, and went weak. She knelt slowly and rubbed at the dirt-and-rust encrusted hilt. An intricately curved, curlique design began to show. She swallowed. There was more design than dirt, she soon found as she rubbed at it. It looked Spanish, and it for sure was very old.

"What's a corn ado?" Laurel asked.

"Coronado was a 'who' not a 'what'," Jessamyn said in a near whisper; her eyes were feverish-looking with the excitement of discovery.

Willow sat back on her heels. "Coronado was a Spanish explorer," she said. "He was here in Kansas back in. . . ." She scratched her head, trying to think.

"Fifteen forty-one," Jessy, who'd studied Kansas history more recently, said. "He was searching for the Seven Cities of Cibola—he thought he would find emeralds and gold, but he didn't. He found Kansas, though, and the Grand Canyon, and lots of other things."

"Wait!" Walsh said with a gulp. "You mean this sword maybe belonged to this Spanish explorer and he lost it right here?"

Willow nodded. "It could have happened. It could have been his sword, or maybe it belonged to one of Coronado's men. I'd bet anybody that's where it came from, Spain. If it did, it's—it's nearly four-hundred years old. Adan," Willow took a deep breath, "that sword is probably worth a lot."

Adan smiled, but didn't say anything. Walsh began to hop about, laughing, punching the air with his fists. "Whoopee!" he yelled. "Adan, you can buy your old Daisy air rifle you been wantin'. An' I'll get me a shotgun if Papa says I can have one—"

"Dresses!" Jessamyn practically sang, doing an exotic flying ballet step in the twilight-purpled barnyard. It was easy to forget that she wore a food-spotted, faded cotton dress as she cried, "Blue velvet, white dotted Swiss, rose-colored satin—"

"Balderdash," Willow broke in drily when she'd had enough. "We'll put a down payment on The Ranch, that's what we'll do." She looked to Adan to agree, but he ignored everyone and picked up the sword. He couldn't have cradled a baby more lovingly in his arms. They trooped behind him to the house.

"Did you see Adan's sword, Mama?" Willow asked as she passed Mama, who was kneading a big yellow lump of fresh-churned butter on the butter board.

Mama looked up, seeming both startled and pleased that Willow had spoken to her. "He show it to me earlier," she answered with a smile. "*Bien.* Is beautiful, beautiful."

They crowded into the boys' lean-to bedroom, trying not to trip baby Mitty who waddled and fell and picked herself up again, clinging to their legs.

"What are you doing?" Walsh puzzled, as Adan went straight to the side wall, reached up, and tore down two magazine pictures fastened there with oversized spike nails. The nails were about two feet apart, and there was a unified gasp as Adan lifted the sword and rested it on the spikes.

"You're wasting time," Willow chided as Adan flopped back on his bed, hands clasped behind his head, looking lovingly at his prize on the wall. "What'd you put it up there for?"

"I'm gonna admire it," Adan said with a wide grin, "just admire, and admire, and admire."

"But only for a little while," Walsh coaxed, "we're gonna buy them guns, remember, Adan? You want that Daisy air rifle bad, don't forget."

Willow leaned over the bed to look Adan squarely in the eyes. "We ought to take the sword to Seena tonight, and talk to—to Melinda Lewis's dad, you know; some of the businessmen in town who could put us in touch with somebody who buys rare things. There's no time to lose. That sword is a collector's dream, you can bet. Somebody will pay dear for it, Adan. Ask any price, you'd probably get it."

"Ain't sellin' the sword," he said, his smile still proud.

"What?" Walsh squealed like a hurt pig. "What d'you mean, Adan?"

Jessy said nothing but her hands were clasped in front of her as though in desperate prayer.

Laurel asked for all of them, "What are you going to do with your Corn Ado sword, Adan?"

His scrawny chest rose and fell in a contented sigh. "I told you." His voice was reverent. "I'm gonna admire it. I'm keepin' it right there on the wall all my life. When I die," he said expansively, "that sword will belong to my boy. And when my boy dies, the sword will go to his boy, and when—"

"That's enough!" Willow cried, "all right, that's enough." From Adan's expression, his mind was made up, permanent. All this time he'd dug for treasure so he could buy things he wanted badly. The time was here, but Adan loved the sword more than anything he could buy with money from selling it!

It wasn't any surprise to her, Willow decided.

It was like the selfish scamp to want to keep the sword himself, not help buy The Ranch. Wasn't it always something like that?

On the other hand, for weeks after Adan dug up the Spanish sword, Willow couldn't help hoping he might change his mind about selling it. Instead, it seemed to mean more to him each passing day. Bitterly disgusted, Willow admitted to herself that when all of them were old men and women, Adan, with little doubt, would still have Coronado's sword among his dearest possessions. There wasn't a thing any of them could do about it.

Again, always, it was hard work and the alfalfa that would get them over the hump so they could buy The Ranch. Willow noticed Papa out in the hayfield several times of late, under a scorching sun, brushing his hands through the seed tops, crushing the gray-green stems in his fist, sniffing the alfalfa with growing satisfaction on his face.

Papa announced he would begin mowing the second week in June. While he was mowing, he said, Willow must go to Seena and hire two good men to come help with the stacking and hauling.

"*Non,*" Mama protested, "you not send young girl to hire men."

"Walsh can go along with Willow." Papa settled it with an impatient wave of his hand. "He can ride my Dulcie, and Willow can ride her Eagle pony. They do fine," he said, looking at Willow and Walsh, "and I get at my mowing."

Mama still didn't like the idea. "Look men in the eyes." She secretly gave Willow instructions the night before they were to go into Seena. "Don't hire men who look like they drink the—the *whiskey*." Mama's voice sank almost out of hearing simply saying the word.

"I'll hire the best I can find," Willow told her.

There was a summery tang in the air and dew still on the grass early next morning as Willow and Walsh got ready to ride out. Willow asked Papa one more time, "Are you sure we will earn enough to pay a hay crew and still have enough to—"

Papa reached up and hesitated before patting her hand holding the reins. "Daughter, we got best crop of alfalfa I ever see. Sooner we get first crop mowed and off the field, sooner second crop come on."

"All right, Papa." Willow managed a smile. "Better let you get to the mowing, then. Going to be another scorcher today—don't think it cooled off much last night." Willow lifted Eagle's reins and clicked her tongue. She looked at Walsh as they rode out onto the road. "You still got jam on your face," she told him. "Better wipe it off before we get to town."

In Seena, with saddles creaking and their horses' hooves clopping on the dusty brick street, Willow and Walsh rode slowly past Mr. Lewis's bank, then the general store. Willow took a good look at two men seated on the bench in front of the store. She shook her head. They were a couple of codgers who had probably worked on hay crews in days gone and knew their stuff, but they were too old now.

They passed the cafe and a delicious whiff of frying potatoes, boiling coffee, and hotcakes came floating out on the morning air. If she didn't find the men where she expected to, at the railroad depot, she would come back to the cafe and ask there, Willow decided.

Jarma Walbridge's father was opening the door to his newspaper office as they rode past, going north. Walsh waved, but the editor had something on his mind. Anyway, he didn't seem to see them.

As they approached the railroad depot, a simple, weathered building by the tracks just to one side of the giant grain elevators, Willow's brow knit anxiously. There wasn't a whole lot of activity here this morning. She had hoped to find her crew among the homeless, returned soldiers who spent their nights on the depot benches. She'd seen a lot more of them about in past months on her way to school than she could see this morning. Maybe they were off across the country, riding the freight trains.

Holding Eagle away from the glinting tracks where the pony might stumble and injure a leg, Willow rode slowly up and back, close in front of the depot. Although she pretended idle indifference, her eyes missed little. On an empty handcar, one man lay snoring loudly. As she passed the dirty unshaven form curled like a baby on the flat top of the handcar, Willow could smell a bitter odor that told her he was one of those men Mama didn't want her to bring home.

Walsh cleared his throat, and when Willow looked, Walsh nodded his head in the direction of another man seated on a bench folding his clothes neatly into a battered duffle bag. The man looked sober and clean, but the strong morning sunshine showed him to be too thin and sickly to be much help to them. Willow shook her head, *no*.

That left the two men in faded, worn olive drab, washing their faces by the water tank. Willow rode up to them and saw with relief that both men were fairly young. The shorter, stocky one reminded her of Walsh, except for his wild red hair. He looked strong, steady, as if he could hold out under long hours of work. The dark slim gent had wide shoulders and nice big hands. But was either man smart enough in the head to load a haywagon right so the hayload didn't shift and fall off? Only one way to find out, Willow decided, taking a deep breath.

"You fellas looking for work by any chance?" she asked.

They whirled at the same time and looked at Willow in surprise, then faint disappointment when they saw that she was a girl. The dark, broad-shouldered man grinned, showing a mouthful of white teeth in his tan face. "What's the job, sweetheart, pickin' pansies?"

The short soldier, mock eagerness in his bright blue eyes, asked, "You want us to sell lemonade?"

He ran a comb quickly through his wet red hair. "Let's go!"

Willow, her cheeks hot, put down a desire to ride away and forget the whole thing. "We're looking for a hay crew," she said. "Either of you done any farmwork?"

The soldiers looked at one another and laughed, then sobered. The tall one spread his hands wide and explained, "Both of us joined the army to get off the farm, miss. But we're needin' work bad, and we're hungry enough to give farmin' another go, at least for a while. Right, Red?"

"Whoa, wait a minute, Dan," Red said. "You young'uns tell the gospel truth now, does your mama set a good table?"

"My ma fries chicken that'll melt in your mouth," Walsh, the eating expert, was quick to answer, "and our sister Jessy makes custard pies you'll remember and want more of the rest of your lives."

Willow backed up her brother's words with a curt nod.

The soldier named Dan blew out a long breath. "You got a crew," he said. "I ain't had a good home-cooked farm dinner since I snuck off from home to join the army four years ago."

Red agreed, "I don't even care to hear what wages you're payin'. When do you want us, and where's your place?"

"Come out around the last day of June—no, maybe you better make it a day or two early, let's say the twenty-eighth. Our name is Faber, I'm Willow and my brother, here, is Walsh. To get to The Ranch, our place, you take the main road straight east from town. We're the second place on the right. You'll see an old stone-walled well out by the road— you see, our place once was a pony express station," Willow added with deep pride.

"We'll be there." Dan walked over and reached up a hand to Willow. As he took hers, a strange expression crossed his face, and he turned her palm up and whistled. "Compared to you, I think we had it easy in the war," he said. "Will you look at them callouses!"

"We're fixin' to buy The Ranch, we only rent it now," she said, pulling her hand back, "it takes a lot of hard work."

"Sis is tough. And meaner'n Old Ned," Walsh cautioned the soldiers, "and gettin' meaner every day. Wait'll she starts crackin' the whip over you." It was plain to all of them that Walsh was not making a joke.

Willow's face turned hot clear into the roots of her hair. "C'mon, Walsh," she growled a threat, "before I start telling them how pretty you look in a yellow dress." She urged Eagle into a trot and shouted over her shoulder, "You'll remember to come out around the twenty-eighth or so?"

"You bet!" Dan shouted, waving.

Red ran a few steps after them. He cupped his hands around his mouth and yelled, "Tell your Mama

I just love biscuits and gravy with my fried chicken, y'all hear? Yummeee!"

"All right," Willow shouted back. "Be seeing you."

fourteen

R ED and Dan will come," Willow insisted when the men hadn't shown up by supper-time on June twenty-eighth. "You could tell, they were good men. They gave me their promise. There's nothing to worry about; they'll be here by morning." Papa looked doubtful, but Willow would not admit to her own worry. The soldiers had to come help them tomorrow. The hay was cut, wind-rowed, dry, ready.

Papa nodded, deep lines etched in his face be-hind his after-supper pipe. "They better, *yah*. We put these two men you hire at the barn to unload hay. Hope they know how to use hayfork, not spill most of load getting it up into loft. You and me, daughter, work in field, pitching. Walsh can drive team and work on the wagon to keep load balanced, even." Papa shook his head in worry. "Another team and wagon, more men, would be good—we got lot of alfalfa to put up. But . . . we get by."

"At least we don't have to worry about rain," Walsh blurted out, "hot as it is." Beads of perspira-tion were shining on his face.

"Listen, dummy, the weather could change just

like that," Willow said with a snap of her fingers. "We got to get the hay in, now."

"No fuss, no fuss," Mama implored. "Too hot for fighting so. Temperature over a hundred for three days now." Mama, washing dishes at the worktable, looked as if she could melt into the dishpan. "Jess," Mama spoke to Jessamyn who worked near her, spreading chocolate icing on a yellow cake, "did you put cottage cheese we make in well to keep cool? Did you see we have plenty thick cream if men want it for pies?"

Jessamyn murmured something. She wiped the perspiration from her brow with the tail of her apron. "Everything is ready. Bread and pies, fried chicken, meat loaves, this cake. Now," she said with a sigh, "I think I'll lay down and die from this heat."

"You should work in the field all day," Willow admonished her sister. "The heat out there is like the fires of you-know-where. Sometimes, I feel like my hair would burn off my head if I didn't have a hat on." She staggered up from her chair and yawned. "Going to bed. If Red and Dan come pretty soon, is somebody going to tell them they can sleep in the barn?"

"I stay up, tell them," Mama said. "I make mulberry preserves tonight, berries not keep any longer."

In her room, Willow stripped off her clothes that were salt-stiff from perspiring so badly. She pulled a thin nightgown down over her body, thinking it was like dressing a bony skeleton. She'd gotten too thin for prettiness this past year, but if that's what it took to buy The Ranch, it made no matter to her. With a sigh, she sank onto her bed, on top of the blankets, and was asleep in minutes.

All too soon, Mama shook her awake and told Willow it was time for breakfast. Willow crept off the bed and got into her workclothes with her eyes mostly closed. At the wash bench in the kitchen she washed in water already soapy from use by Mama and Papa. She touched the rough towel to her face gingerly. Never could she remember being this sunburned and sore.

More awake now, Willow saw that Papa had eaten and gone outside. Walsh had gone out, too, judging by the second dirty plate. "Is Papa out with Red and Dan? Did they come in last night, or this morning?" Willow felt a stir of excitement at their big day, today, in spite of the fatigue that never seemed to leave her bones these days.

Mama frowned. She looked awfully tired, herself. "They not come. Not last night. Not this morning. Papa so worry he sick."

Willow let the bad news sink in, her heart drumming with panic. "They—Red and Dan—didn't come at all?"

Mama shook her head. She pulled out a chair, dropped into it, then lay her head on her arms folded on the table. "You were up all night, Mama?" Willow asked. Not waiting for an answer, she took her plate of breakfast from the warming oven and sat down across from Mama. She ate without tasting, trying to see a way out of their predicament.

"They'll come," she said finally. "I know Red and Dan will show up. They have to." She laughed, to herself mostly, an odd, hollow sound. "It's still dark outside, it isn't even five o'clock yet. They'll show up. We'll get started, but they'll come before long."

When Red and Dan hadn't shown up by mid-morning, Adan, surprisingly, offered to help. Papa gave the ten-year-old the job of spreading the hay to the edges of the wagon and driving the team, then, to the next row of windrowed hay. This freed Walsh to help Willow and Papa pitch the hay onto the wagon.

The heavy, stifling heat made quick motion impossible. It was like standing still, Willow thought; they crawled along so slow, made so little progress across the giant field. They had to keep on, though. And the soldiers would come.

When the sun was almost directly overhead, Willow and Papa, Walsh and Adan were all desperate for their noon rest and meal. In the last moment, Walsh tiredly swung a last forkful of hay onto the wagon, not looking. It spilled all over Adan, standing on the load, and was full of bumblebees. They fought the bees with their hats, but Adan received several stings. Tears were making streams through the dust on Adan's red face when he hopped off the wagon and followed the others to the house for dinner.

Before they ate, a mud plaster was made and spread on Adan's hands and face until he looked like a tar baby. Still, he hurt bad, Willow could see it. "You don't need to help us this afternoon." Beyond those few words, Willow could muster no further feelings.

Red and Dan did not show up at noon, although Willow kept looking toward the door while they ate. When she, Papa, and Walsh returned to the hayfield, without Adan, Willow was shocked to find that the handle of her pitchfork was as hot to the touch as a stove lid over a fire. There was no relief from the unmerciful sun; the afternoon wore on. The wind blew constantly, but was so heat-filled, it brought no comfort.

"Can't we speed up a little?" Willow croaked once. Neither Papa nor Walsh answered her. They didn't even look in her direction. She thought fretfully that they should be getting the work done twice, three times faster than they were. But the work went grindingly slow, as they loaded the hayrack, drove it to the barn, unloaded it with the hayfork, up into the barn, then back to the hay in the field. To Willow, the size of the field was beginning to look like half the world.

Next day the heat was worse. Willow saw that it was bothering Papa even more than her and Walsh. Papa's movements became like those of an old, old man. Often his hand went up to his head, to the spot where the kaffir corn knife had struck him.

They emptied the first load of hay at the barn and were ready to drive back to the field, when Papa turned uncertainly to Willow, staring at her as though he couldn't quite see her. "We go to—to h-house," he mumbled after a moment. "Too h-hot. M-my head . . ." Papa reeled and almost fell, then caught himself on the side of the wagon. He leaned there for a bit, then straightened. "Walsh, help me to house."

Willow watched as Walsh got a shoulder under Papa's arm and began to move him with stumbling steps across the stubbled field.

Papa spoke to her over his shoulder, "Y-you come in, too, daughter." His look studied her for an instant. "Don't be stubborn, girl."

Willow stayed where she was, without answering, and watched them go. There was work to be done. She climbed onto the wagon, picked up the lines, and clucked the team into motion, to the waiting windrowed hay that looked like long fat green pillows baking in the sun. Willow pitched several forkfuls onto one side of the rack, then went to the other side and pitched on an equal amount there. Then, she climbed on the wagon and spread the hay load even. It was going to take forever, but if she had to get the hay in alone, she would get the hay in alone.

An hour, maybe two passed; Willow was losing track of time. Papa and Walsh did not come back to the hayfield. Willow's head hurt; her motions had become as automatic as a conditioned machine. She worked on. Her sweaty clothing stuck to her skin uncomfortably, the salt from her perspiration bit into all the cuts and scratches the stickery hay had made on her hands and face.

A while later, Willow believed she could see an auto parked out on the road, at the edge of the field. Red and Dan? She squinted, trying to see through the blue haze in front of her eyes. It was a lone figure— Auberta Steele—stomping toward her. Willow had a fleeting wish to share the palm fan that Auberta whipped back and forth before her mannish face.

"What are you doing out here?" Auberta Steele gaped. "This is killing weather, don't you know you got to have help? Where's your Papa? Your brothers? Your Pa told me he was goin' to hire a hay crew."

"Hir-hired a coup-couple soldiers," Willow told her. "Supposed to've come other night, didn't get here, yet. They're c-comin'."

The spinster was silent a moment, then her leathery face broke into a sudden, taunting, know-it-all smile. "You ain't heard out here, have you?" she chortled. "The war ended *official* yesterday, in France. The whole town of Seena is celebrating, going crazy, like they did last November eleventh when the Germans first surrendered. They're throwing a real wingding, again. That's where your soldier

boys are, girl. Celebratin', whooping it up, in Seena."
She cackled. "They ain't in no condition to work
in no hayfield today, believe me."

Willow stared at Auberta Steele, weaved, shook
her aching head to rid the dark that threatened.
"N-not c-coming?"

Auberta Steele, fluttering her fan, still smiling,
shook her head. "If you've got the sense God gave
you, girl, you'll get in out of this sun." She turned
to leave. Willow overheard the spinster mumble,
"They hadn't ought to be on this place, nohow.
Maybe now . . . !"

Auberta Steele vanished into the blue haze while
Willow watched. Should she go to the house? Let
Auberta have The Ranch, have it all, have her life?
Willow turned blindly and struck her pitchfork into
a shock of hay and lifted it slowly onto the rack.
They could get the hay in while taking naps in the
shade? How could they buy The Ranch without the
alfalfa money? Did the rest of them forget? Did
Mama and Papa and the kids want to move again in
a few months, another ramshackle place—somewhere
—and move and move and move—till they turned
to dust?

Jessamyn came out to the field. Willow looked
at her dully. Her sister's sandy hair and faded blue
dress were so damp with sweat she looked as if someone had thrown water on her. Jessy's usually pretty
face was hard to see, just a blot. "Mama and Papa

says you're to come to the house right now, Willow."
Willow waved her away as she might a mirage she
didn't believe. Jessy waited awhile, staring at Willow,
then she turned and left.

Watching her go, Willow's face screwed up into
a hard squint. She giggled hollowly. Funny, Jessamyn
looked for all the world like a mermaid swimming
off into a bluish yellow sea!

Oh, how her head hurt. Even with her straw
hat, the sun was splitting her head in two, like a too-
ripe plum. Willow turned back to work. They had
to get the hay in hay in hay in. . . .

"H-hup," Willow whispered to the team, "get
on there." Standing on the ground, Willow tried to
follow the team and wagon to the next windrow,
but her silly legs—wouldn't—move. "What—?" she
whispered as the hayfield, the mules, the hayrack, all
began to sway, around, around, in wide, dizzying
circles. The lines slipped from her fingers. "Whoa,"
Willow pleaded in a soundless whisper. "Whoa,
world." But the dark reached up, gathered her in.
Cut grass scratched her cheek when she hit the
ground; an insect crawled across her closed eyelids.
Then Willow knew no more.

For the next hours, days, unmeasurable time, headache was like a wedge in Willow's skull. When pain
and vomiting allowed, she sank into welcome sleep
with no wish to come out.

She heard someone, Papa, tell her, "You got sunstroke, daughter, but you get better, *yah*." Willow made an effort to focus her eyes on the face above her; it was too hard to do, she closed her eyes.

Mama came, with a cup of warm salt water for her to drink. "The headache, she is better? Please drink, *ma chérie*, you must help us make you better." Willow looked at her mother, couldn't see, didn't move. Mama placed a hand at the back of Willow's neck, raised her, poured the salt water between her unresisting lips.

Papa clutched Willow's limp hand, a glitter of tears in his faded blue eyes. "I tell you over and over, but you don't listen, I think," he said. "Daughter, alfalfa is all in! I got money, I pay Abrahams, I got papers for your Ranch. Is what you want, what you always want, *yah?*"

Willow could see and hear Papa's concern, but she couldn't summon a response. She felt dead. Her feelings, caring, were gone, as if the sun had burned them out of her that day in the hayfield. All the sun had left to her was pain. Pain, like another being, had taken over her body. Willow closed her eyes, but it didn't shut out the pain that drummed on in her head.

Willow was aware, but scarcely heeded, that some member of the family stood by her bed, fanning her, much of the time. Jessamyn and Mama came and went with wet cloths for her head. They brought special tidbits of food she could not get down. Why did they fuss so? As though something mattered. Nothing mattered, nothing.

In a voice meant to excite, Jessamyn told Willow, "Your soldiers, Red and Dan, finally came, you know. They were late, but they came. Frank Tucker and Doretta came, too, with boys and girls from your class, when they heard. All the neighbors came and helped. You should have seen them, sister. The temperature dropped a few degrees—if only you'd waited . . ." Jessy's voice broke, she fell silent.

Willow heard. She tried to think why it was that getting The Ranch, the hay in, had been important. It hurt too much to think. She couldn't remember. It didn't matter.

Laurel came one afternoon to tell Willow, "I found you, I got help when you almost died in the hayfield." She looked at Willow expectantly, waiting for Willow's answer, her thanks. When Willow looked at her, through eyes veiled with pain, saying nothing, Laurel ran sobbing to the family in the next room. "Willow is a mean ol' whip," the little girl cried. "She won't talk to me, and I let my doll Amanda sleep with her. Willow used to love me."

Early one dawn, Willow woke hearing a catbird singing a strong sweet song just outside her window. It was like the catbird had something to do with her heart, the trilling seemed to have set it beating again, after it had been long stopped. Willow opened her eyes slowly, with caution for the fearful, terrible pain. None. The headache was gone. She blinked, looked about gradually, seeing her surroundings in the dawn gloom as though she'd just been born this fresh new moment.

A huge ghostly bouquet of cabbage roses in a jar sat on the bureau. She recognized them from the Abrahams' front yard. Frank must have brought them. Her funny friend. Willow stirred for a better look, and the scent of lilacs filled her nose. She smiled. Mama was using her best sheets, those she kept scented with lilac in a trunk, put away for good, using them for her! Willow's glance grew gentle, seeing Papa's cob pipe on the table by the door. He took it from his mouth only at the last moment each night. He must have been sitting up with her. Poor Papa, good Papa.

She wanted to see, must see, the morning come. Willow struggled up to a sitting position. The silver dawn outside turned pale pink very slowly, now it was yellowing. Now the room filled with pale gold light. It sure was the prettiest thing. Willow looked down, her eyes smarting. There, on a chair by her bed, lay an official-looking paper.

Willow hesitated, drew a deep breath, and picked it up. Her fingers trembled. It was Papa's copy of the agreement to buy The Ranch; there was his crudely scrawled signature, *Karl Faber*, and there Eliot and Egbert Abraham's signatures, too. It had happened. . . . Willow's eyes burned unbearably for a full minute before the tears came, a warm rushing flood.

She remembered now something Papa had said to her sometime, in the days past. What was it—? Yes, Papa had told her, "When my hope to own our own land is gone, you come along, daughter, growing up, wanting the same. You give me my hope back. I love you for that, girl, I do."

It had happened.

But hadn't it almost cost too much, her wanting The Ranch so bad? Too much. Hadn't the family come near to hating her, almost, for her whip-driving ways? Walsh and Adan getting lost in the snowstorm—that was her fault; they so easily could have died that night. And the boys and girls at school—a minute or two, here and there, to be more friendly wouldn't have hurt. If she'd really tried, things would have been different, sooner. Frank. He ought to have his head examined for liking her at all. She'd like to see him today, her funny friend. Maybe he would come if someone went to tell him.

One more thing—maybe the worst—she'd gotten to be so rough, hard. Rude, an awful lot like that Auberta Steele. Ugh! She'd never wanted that to happen! It was mostly on the outside, maybe; her most inside self wasn't that way, couldn't be like that.

Willow dried her tears. A willow didn't have to be a whip. A willow could give in the wind, too, just a little, when it was needed. Yes. This Willow was going to be like that from now on.

Fresh, happy tears spurted from Willow's eyes when she again fingered the document with Papa's dear scrawl on it. Then, she laughed; strong feelings, like alfalfa seeds bursting in rich warm earth, stirred in her heart. They had done it! A wonder, they really had! *Theirs.* The Ranch was Faber land, now, to live and die on till the end of time. For keeps through thick and thin.

With shaking hands, Willow took off the sheet that covered her. "Mama?" she called. "Papa?" She stepped out on the floor and swayed there. "Hey, Walsh," she yelled, "old brother? And you, Adan, you up? Clay? Jessy, sister, and you, you sweetie, Laurel? Know what? We got The Ranch!"

Shouting it, over and over, Willow took her first tentative steps in more than a week. Making so much noise herself, she scarcely heard the thudding footsteps crossing the floors of the old stagecoach-station house, the surprised shouts in return, the sleepy laughter—echoes of joy.